Could

Rene stuffed his handkerchief into his front pocket. He shifted his gaze from her face to the front of the school. Marisa could tell that the nerd wasn't familiar with her kind of school, one with security guards who themselves looked like thugs.

"Who's that? Einstein?" A crew of girls bent over, holding their sides laughing.

"Come down here and say that! We can chunk right here!" Marisa barked. Her hands curled into fists and then uncurled, each of her long fingernails like daggers.

None of the girls moved, but none stopped laughing. They guffawed and did a dance around the backpacks at their feet.

"Don't worry about me," Rene said. "People are always picking on me."

Marisa winced at his admission. "They wouldn't pick on you if I was around. They would show you some respect." She was surprised by her proclamation. She hadn't known the nerd more than five minutes and yet she was defending him.

Other Books by Gary Soto

Mercy on These Teenage Chimps
A Fire in My Hands
Help Wanted: Stories
The Afterlife
Petty Crimes
Buried Onions
Novio Boy: A Play
Canto familiar
Jesse
Local News
Pacific Crossing
Neighborhood Odes
Taking Sides
Baseball in April and Other Stories

Accidental LOVE

Gary Soto

HARCOURT, INC.
Orlando Austin New York San Diego London

www.HarcourtBooks.com

First Harcourt paperback edition 2008

The Library of Congress has cataloged the hardcover edition as follows:
Soto, Gary.
Accidental love/Gary Soto.
p. cm.
Summary: After unexpectedly falling in love with a "nerdy" boy, fourteen-year-old Marisa works to change her life by transferring to another school, altering some of her behavior, and losing weight.
[1. Love—Fiction. 2. Schools—Fiction. 3. Overweight persons—Fiction. 4. Hispanic Americans—Fiction.] I. Title.
PZ7.S7242Acc 2006
[Fic]—dc22 2004029900
ISBN 978-0-15-205497-7
ISBN 978-0-15-206113-5 pb

Text set in Melior
Designed by April Ward

C E G H F D B

Printed in the United States of America

For Armando Ramirez
and the good folks
at Half Moon Bay Library

Accidental LOVE

Chapter

At fourteen Marisa welcomed any excuse to miss school. But today she had a good reason for cutting class. Alicia, her best friend, lay in the hospital with a broken leg and a broken heart, all because her boyfriend had crashed his parents' car when a tire blew. The leg had broken in the crash, but her heart had broken when the glove compartment opened on impact and shot out a photo of stupid Roberto with his arm around another girl.

Marisa was off to give her homegirl a meaningful hug. "He's such a shisty rat," she growled as she pictured that no-good Roberto, an average-looking fool whose fingers were always orange from Cheetos. She, too, savored that junk food snack, but—she argued—at least she always licked her fingers clean.

But not him! Stupid jerk! Big *pendejo*! How could Alicia stand his face? She was always treating him to food and paying for gas for their car rides into the country.

Marisa's anger was deflected to a passing station wagon that nearly hit her as she started across the street. "You *estúpido*!" she spat as she threw her hands into the air in anger. The pair of eyes she saw in the rearview mirror were old and could have belonged to any of her six aunts. *Ay, Chihuahua,* how Marisa's grandmother bore children, all female, all large, all different as pepper from salt. Marisa admonished herself for yelling at the elderly driver. "Maybe it was one of *mis tías,*" she told herself, and her rage dissolved. Her thoughts returned to Alicia tucked away in a hospital bed and then quickly to Roberto, the rat. *If my boyfriend was cheating on me*...She was brooding when she remembered that she didn't have a boyfriend. So what was the worry? She found herself shrugging and thinking she'd never have a boyfriend as she peeked at her stomach with its roll of fat.

"Room 438," she told herself as the salmon-colored hospital came into view. "That's where my homegirl is. She's gonna be hecka surprised." Marisa swallowed her fear. Hospitals were where you went to die. She remembered Grandma Olga's last days. Her grandmother, struggling with cancer, rolled from her side to her stomach to sitting on the bed and dangling her rope-thin legs. Dying, Marisa had thought then, was a matter of getting comfortable.

Marisa rode up in an elevator between two male nurses with paper bootees on their shoes. She herself had considered becoming a nurse, but that was years before, when she had dolls whose arms would fall off, and she would stick the arms back on only to have them fall off again. The dolls, she remembered, lay under her bed, their eyes open but not taking in a whole lot.

The elevator opened with a sigh. Marisa stepped out, glancing slowly left and then right. "Room 438," she muttered as she cut a glance to a man in a wheelchair pushing himself up the hallway by the strength of his thin arms. A bottle of clear fluid hung on a steel pole behind him, and clear tubes were delivering that fluid into his arms.

Marisa grimaced. She would hate to have something stabbed in her all day. *Does it hurt like a pinch?* she wondered. *A bee sting?*

When she located the room, Alicia was staring gloomily toward the ceiling. For a moment Marisa figured that Alicia was appealing to God in heaven. But as she stepped inside, she realized that Alicia's eyes were raised to a muted television. On the screen some carpenter was carrying a sheet of plywood over his head. It was a boring home-decorating show, the kind her mother liked to watch on Saturday afternoons.

"Hey, girl!" Marisa greeted loudly.

Alicia lowered her eyes to her friend, and for a few seconds her face was expressionless. Then it slowly blossomed with a smile. Her eyes narrowed into little slits of light.

"Marisa," Alicia greeted in return. She raised a feeble hand and Marisa grasped her friend's hand and gave it a loving squeeze, then smothered Alicia with a hug.

"How's it? Your *pata*?" Marisa asked as she sat on the edge of the bed.

"It's not my leg," Alicia replied, and rapped her heart as if it were a door. "It's this that's hurting."

Marisa's eyes flashed as her mind fluttered with the image of Roberto. Sure, he got in trouble with his parents for crashing the car, but wasn't Alicia worse off?

"I told you he was no good," Marisa offered in judgment. "Is your mom really mad?" Alicia's mother was an accountant and was not only good at numbers but also at keeping tabs on her daughter's whereabouts.

"A little bit. Actually, a lot," Alicia answered

weakly. Her tiny hands squeezed her blanket. Marisa, a big girl whose shadow covered other people's when they walked together, couldn't help but think of Alicia as a little doll. She couldn't keep herself from saying, "You look so tiny, girl."

"I am tiny."

This truth made Marisa smolder. *How dare Roberto cheat on my little homegirl!* How she would love to get him into a headlock and bounce his head off a wall. She had watched enough wrestling on TV to know how to do it.

"My mom says I can't see him anymore."

"My mom would be hecka mad," Marisa said. "And my dad—" She shrugged. She wasn't clear how her dad would view such a tragedy. He was a lot more carefree. But her mom? She pictured her mother at the stove smashing beans into *refritos* and yelling over the radio that her daughter was headed down the wrong road, blah, blah, blah.

"What are you doing here? How come you're not at school?" Alicia asked.

"Seeing you," Marisa replied. "I just walked right out of school and two miles to get here." She pinched her stomach. "I'm gonna start losing weight."

"You look good."

"¡Mentirosa!" Marisa swiped a light slap on her friend's arm. She repeated how she had bounced

down the stairs of second-floor East Hall and walked out of Washington High School during morning break. The security guard had even waved good-bye. That was how much they didn't care.

Alicia placed a hand over her mouth and laughed. "You're *mala.* Your mom and dad's going to find out."

"So?" But Marisa was worried. Her mom had threatened that if she got in trouble again at school—she had been suspended for a week for fighting over lip gloss she had lent some girl—she was going to send her away to live with one of her aunts. Marisa didn't want to get in trouble again, but the idea of going to a new school appealed to her. She knew that she would miss a few friends, but she could always depend on her cell phone. Each month she was loaded with free minutes.

Alicia's eyes suddenly filled and two lines of tears raced down her cheeks.

Marisa thumbed the salty track making its way down to the left side of Alicia's chin, and she was amazed how cool the tear was. If *she* were crying, her tears would be as hot as motor oil.

"Do you want me to hit him?" Marisa asked. Her hand was closed into a rock-hard fist.

"Who?" Alicia asked, sounding like a sad owl.

"Roberto!" Roberto was tall but lanky. Marisa

imagined that she could lower her shoulder and bulldoze him into the lockers and follow up with a smacking slap to his face. This, too, she had learned from watching wrestling. Who said TV was a waste of time?

"No," Alicia said, then pouted like a fish. "I don't need him."

"You go, girl." Marisa smiled and leaned her face into her friend's shoulder. They hugged and told each other how they couldn't depend on anyone except each other. Marisa's own tears began to roll hot from her eyes. But the girls stopped hugging when Marisa heard a voice behind her. The voice belonged to someone Marisa knew. Her mother!

Busted! Marisa thought as she swiped away the tears from her eyes and sat up.

"Hi, Mrs. Rodriguez," Alicia greeted. "I asked Marisa to come and see me."

Marisa's mother stood with her hands propped on her hips. Her eyes narrowed darkly. She seemed to weigh whether Alicia was telling the truth. She shook her head, jangling her earrings, and made her judgment. "You girls are lying. Marisa's skipping school. You think I was born yesterday?"

Marisa opened her mouth, forging the image of a daughter shocked that a parent—a mother, of all people!—didn't believe her. She raised her hands to her chest as if to say, "You mean me?" She would have stamped her foot dramatically in protest to her mother's verdict, but she was sitting on the edge of the high hospital bed. Her feet didn't touch the floor.

"Don't say anything that I can use against you later," her mother warned, a storm beginning to rage inside her.

Her mother sounded like the police. And to Marisa, she *was* the police with her own court and punishment.

"It's my fault, Mrs. Rodriguez," Alicia piped up. "I told her to come."

Marisa's mother ignored her as she repeated the lie, obvious because Marisa volunteered a truth: "Nah, I came on my own, Mom. It's my fault."

"I'll be talking to you later," her mother told Marisa. "Aren't you sorry I decided to come visit Alicia myself?" She turned her hard gaze from her daughter to Alicia. Her mother's eyes softened, the storm inside subsiding. "How are you, *mi'ja*?"

"It's only a fracture," Alicia replied with her hand on her heart. "The doctor is releasing me tomorrow."

"Cool!" Marisa crowed.

Marisa's mother frowned at her daughter. She then turned her attention back to Alicia and asked if the doctor had prescribed pain pills and how long the leg would be in a cast. She didn't ask about the boy who had been driving the car when the accident occurred.

"I got some pills and it really don't hurt so bad. It's just that it itches." Alica pulled up the bedsheet and revealed a blue cast that came up to her thigh. She knocked on the cast. "It's really hard."

Marisa was curious how Alicia would shower. Wouldn't the cast get soggy and fall off? Instead she asked, "Did they get you some getaway sticks, some crutches?"

"Not yet. Someone's going to teach me to use them today."

They talked mainly about school and family. When Alicia mentioned the fall dance and a tide of tears rose in her eyes, Marisa's mother patted her hand. She produced from her purse a small package of miniature white-powdered doughnuts.

"I know that sweets aren't very good for you," her mother whispered after she gazed back at the door, where occasionally a nurse passed in the hallway. "But these will make you feel better. They're better than pain pills. And forget about the dance. There'll be others."

Marisa was going to snap, "You never buy me doughnuts like that!" But her mouth, which often got her into trouble, closed as quickly as it had opened. She realized that Alicia was hurt and that her mother was displaying her concern.

"Thank you, Mrs. Rodriguez. I love these!" Alicia said. She opened up the package and offered the first doughnut to Marisa.

Marisa was moved. "She's a true friend," she told herself. She took a bite and then offered the rest to Alicia, who opened her mouth and closed it around the doughnut. Some crumbs fell onto the front of Alicia's hospital gown, but she scooped them up. She sucked them down like a vacuum, something Marisa knew that she would do in private but never with anyone looking on. The intimate gesture convinced her that Alicia was the best friend ever.

Marisa's mother refused the doughnuts, but the girls ate until they were gone and both were wishing for glasses of milk to wash them down.

"Okay, let's go," Marisa's mother ordered her daughter as she got off the bed, smoothing her dress.

Marisa raised a hand, as if holding a cell phone to her ear. "Call you later."

Alicia blew her friend a kiss.

Mother and daughter rode the noiseless elevator down. Marisa expected her mother to yell at her, but her mother, looking into a compact and dabbing her mouth with red, red lipstick, instead told her that they had to stop at a repair shop—she had discovered a nail in the front left tire.

Marisa was baffled. Roberto's parents' car had had something wrong with a tire. Now a nail was protruding from a tire on their car. Were tire problems more common than she realized? She was mulling this new mystery when the elevator opened.

Marisa gasped. In front of her stood Roberto, who looked like damaged goods because of the bandages on his head and right forearm. In his good arm he cradled flowers that were at least a day old and already starting to sag. "You shanky dude," she caught herself cursing in her mind. She pushed aside the guy who was with Roberto, both of her hands closed into fists. She couldn't help herself, even as her mother pulled on her and warned, "Marisa, stop!"

Marisa shrugged out of her mother's grip.

"You cheater! She loved you so much!" Marisa yelled. She hauled off and fired a stiff punch into Roberto's iron-flat stomach—she had always suspected that a tapeworm lay curled in there devouring all those bags of Cheetos. The flowers popped out of his arms. She stomped on them and began to thrash him from all angles. Watching all that wrestling on TV was beginning to pay off.

Chapter

It had been six years since Marisa had last been sentenced by her mother to the confines of her bedroom, six years since she had taken a pair of scissors and cut her sleeping cousin's pigtails. She had cut the pigtails because... Marisa couldn't remember why exactly. She could only recall how she'd sat by her bedroom window and watched rain slide down the glass. Her sadness was like the rain—gray, cold, and constant. She was eight then, with a little baby fat that rolled over the elastic waistband of her Cinderella pajamas.

Now that she was fourteen, the baby fat had spread. She lay on her unmade bed bathing her legs in the afternoon sun that cut through the window. She wiggled her toes, their painted red nails chipped in places. She debated with herself whether thumping Roberto had been the right thing to do. But after she took a sip of cream soda, she concluded that the sorry rat deserved such punishment, and then some. He had cheated on her best friend in the whole world.

Her cell phone began to ring, and she searched wildly about her bedroom. Her eyes raked over the chest of drawers cluttered with soda cans, unused bottles of perfume, lipsticks squat as silver bullets, candy wrappers, burger wrappers, CDs of rockers she never listened to anymore, a single sock, a dried bouquet from a wedding, and other assorted trash that she knew she should cram into paper bags before the short journey to the garbage can. Her room was a mess.

"It's probably Alicia," she told herself. However, when she picked up the phone, she heard a guy say, "Rene, it's me, Trung. I can't figure out the problem."

The problem? Marisa was at a loss as to what to say, a new sensation because her mouth was always ready to gush out words.

"You there?" the voice asked. "Rene? You there? Your batteries dead?"

She clicked off her cell phone and looked at it. "Dang," she muttered as she let it roll from her fingers onto her bed, as if it were a gun and she had just committed a horrible act. The cell phone wasn't hers. She bit her lower lip and raised her eyes toward the ceiling. "I bet it belongs to that other guy," she told herself. She recalled the boy who had been with Roberto, the one who had finally pulled her away from him and whose eyeglasses had come off. During the tussle their cell phones had fallen and each must have walked away with the other's.

She called her own cell number, wiggling her toes as she waited for that guy to pick up. But her own rushed voice came on rudely: "YOU leave a message and you speak clearly, you know WHAT I *mean*?" Marisa grimaced at the awkward cadence of her message and the attitude behind her voice. "That's me?" she uttered in disbelief and hung up. She promised herself that once she got her cell phone back she was going to change the greeting.

Her mother rattled the door with a heavy knock. "Marisa!" she yelled.

Marisa sucked her breath and held it.

"MA-RI-SA! It's time to eat!"

Marisa pocketed the cell phone, let her breath out like a deflating balloon, and yelled, "Okay, okay!" She brushed her hair behind her ears, checked her face in the mirror on the wall, and muttered, "She's always on me."

Dinnertime. Marisa's father sat at one end of the

table. He had the eyes of a worker who wakes up before dawn and starts off for the day just as the pinkish sun appears in the east. They were tired, puffy, and half closed. Her father was a carpenter, a man who often returned home with flakes of wood in his thin graying hair. His rough hands were sometimes bleeding, his fingertips puffed from hits with his hammer.

Marisa plopped onto a chair at the kitchen table. The fourth chair, where her brother Ralphie used to sit, held a basket of clean laundry. Her brother had gone away to Bakersfield State. Now it was usually only the three of them, and sometimes Alicia, and sometimes one of the many aunts.

"Hey, Dad," Marisa greeted. She scooted her chair in and picked up her spoon.

Her father wagged his head, his way of saying hi. He was a quiet man who preferred gestures to long-winded sentences.

"Tell him what happened,' her mother started in immediately.

Here we go, Marisa thought, *dinner talk about my wicked, wicked ways.* She played dumb and said, "What?"

"You know 'what.'" Her mother blew on her bowl of *albóndigas.* The surface of the hot broth rippled.

"You mean that I skipped school and went to

see Alicia. I know Dad would go see his best friend if he was in the hospital." She looked at her father, who was dipping a chunk of sourdough bread into his soup. "Huh, Dad?"

"I don't have a best friend," he answered simply.

"Pete," Marisa reminded him. She set her spoon like an oar into her soup and stirred, creating a current that made the peas and chunks of carrots swim in a circle.

"Oh, Pete," her father remarked as he brought a paper napkin to his stubbly face. "He ran away with another woman. Left his wife and kids. How can I be friends with an *hombre* like that?"

"At least he ran away with another woman, not a guy," Marisa replied. Then she wished she could pull back that string of words and push it down her throat. It was rude, she realized, inconsiderate, and—yes—plain dumb.

"That's not funny at all," her mother said.

"Whatever," Marisa said absently. Again she wished she could retract that comment.

"Don't 'whatever' me," her mother scolded. With a large fork like a pitchfork, she stabbed at some bread in the basket and told her husband their daughter had cut school to see Alicia. What did he think of that?

The father slurped his soup but didn't say anything.

Marisa waited for her mother to elaborate on her adventure at the hospital. She waited for her to tell her father how she'd had to chunk it up with Roberto, but her mother didn't bring up the fight outside the elevator. *Bless her,* Marisa thought, *maybe she's really not so bad after all.* Perhaps her father would have grumbled and lectured her by telling her a long story about how when he was a young man he kept his temper by counting to ten in Spanish. This was in Fresno, where young men at street corners fell over like bowling pins. Times then, as now, were dangerous.

"Your friend, Alicia, is she okay?" Marisa's father tore his bread in half and dipped one piece into his soup. He ate with his face close to the bowl.

"She's getting out of the hospital tomorrow," Marisa answered. She slapped her roll with butter before she dipped it into her soup. "She has to use crutches."

"She shouldn't have been with that boy," her mother interjected. "Rafael, I had a nail in the front tire."

"What *chavalo*?" her father asked. "And did you get the tire fixed?"

"Helen's son," Marisa's mother answered. She told them that Rudy at Rudy's Tire and Wheel had fixed the tire himself. She reminded him that Helen was a person she had known when they both worked in a drapery shop.

"I don't know her," her father remarked.

"Yeah, you do, *viejo,*" her mother mumbled with her mouth full. "Helen Lopez. Her husband is the one who started the nursery on Jensen Avenue. They have real nice roses."

Her father answered, "Oh, now I remember." He lifted a glass of water, drank, and set his water glass down.

Marisa could tell that her father didn't remember, not Helen or Helen's husband. He was a poor pretender.

"This soup is good." Marisa hoped that her compliment would steer the conversation away from Roberto the rat. She blew on her soup and nearly spilled it when her cell phone, stuffed in her front pocket, started to ring.

Her father raised his eyes from his bowl. "You got ants in your pants?" He smiled at his feeble joke.

Marisa returned the smile. She excused herself and rushed from the kitchen into the living room and finally the hallway, where she clicked on the cell phone.

"Yeah," she said.

"This is Rene," the voice said.

"I don't know no Rene." She grimaced. *Dang, I sound stupid,* she thought. *Why can't I say things right?*

"We met—," Rene started to say.

"Oh, yeah. At the hospital," she completed. "And you have my cell phone and I've got yours."

Silence. A branch scratched the window on the side of the house. The furnace was kicking on in the basement. Ages of more silence.

"And you want yours back, huh?" Marisa finally asked. She brought a strand of hair into her mouth and began to nibble it like a straw.

"I guess that's why I'm calling."

"Where do you live?" Marisa asked. She could tell that he was a shy person. His voice was small, like a little boy's.

"Do you know where Willow Park is?" he asked. "I live over there, near Hamilton Magnet."

Marisa knew the area. It had nice homes and green, green lawns and its own private security car that circled the neighborhood like a shark. She remembered how she and Alicia had gone trick-or-treating up there and hauled away bags crammed full of wrapped candy bars, not fistfuls of cheap candy, raisins, backyard apples, and walnuts. She remembered devouring the candy until her jaw hurt and chocolate darkened the corners of her mouth.

"That park's too far away. I don't know how I'm going to get your phone to you."

"I got a bike," he replied. "Do you go to Washington with Roberto? I could meet you tomorrow."

"If you want to," she said. "How do you know Roberto, anyway?"

"I tutor him in math."

Marisa cringed at the sound of her mother's voice calling from the kitchen. She was yelling, "MA-RI-SA! You gotta help with the dishes!"

Marisa held the phone away from her mouth. "I'm talking on the phone, Mom!" she screamed in return. When her mother didn't cry, "Then get off the phone," Marisa raised the cell phone back to her ear. "Sorry," she told Rene. "Can you meet at three thirty?"

"How about four thirty?" Rene asked. "I got a chess meeting."

"Chess meeting!" she nearly exclaimed. But she held her tongue and agreed to meet in front of her school. She hung up and stared at the phone, trying to reassemble what the boy looked like. Her memory could only bring up Roberto's startled look when she landed an impressive punch to his gut.

"Dishes!" Marisa's mother yelled.

Marisa returned to the kitchen. She slurped the rest of her soup and nearly fit a whole roll into her mouth before she thought better of it. She wasn't hungry; plus, she could hear her mother's footsteps padding toward the kitchen. Her mother would badger her about eating too much—one bowl of soup should be enough for any girl. She thought for a moment that it was like prisoner's food. Bread and water.

Her mother came into the kitchen. *"Mira,"* she said. She waved something in Marisa's face that at first she thought was a dead bat. "You washed your black sock with the whites."

"I didn't do it," Marisa snapped back.

"What, did the sock walk into the whites and say, 'Bleach me'?" Her mother started to stuff the leftover rolls into a plastic bag.

Marisa plucked the once-black sock from her mother's hand and pushed it into her back pocket like a flag used in flag football.

"*Mi'ja,* I don't want you to cut school again," her mother said softly.

"I won't," Marisa said weakly.

"We want you to do well in school." She hugged her daughter and said that she was a good girl. "You're our only daughter."

To Marisa that was one of the sweetest things her mother had said to her in a long time. Her mother usually told her things to do—pick up clothes, put the milk away—and was constantly warning her about trouble she could get into if she wasn't careful.

"I want to do good, too. I don't want to mess up."

Her mother hugged her and left the kitchen when her husband began wailing that there was something wrong with the remote control.

Marisa gathered the bowls and spoons from the table and carried them to the sink. She turned on the water and waited for it to rise in the plastic tub before she submerged the dinnerware. She squirted dish soap into the steaming tub, pushed her pudgy fingers into rubber gloves, and started on her evening chore. She found herself thinking about that boy with the sweet voice, whose face she could have remembered if she hadn't been so busy pummeling Roberto.

Chapter

Marisa sized up a gangly boy approaching on a bike. He looked familiar, so she guessed he was Rene. He wore dress pants, like the kind her father put on for church, and a plaid button-down shirt with his shirttail tucked in. His eyeglasses were slightly bent on his face. As he pedaled she made out white socks with three red stripes near the top. *Dang, the boy's a nerd,* she thought. Was he really the same one who had been with Roberto?

"Hi," Rene squeaked after he kicked a leg over the bar and glided his bike onto the patchy lawn in front of the school. He brought a handkerchief from his pocket and swabbed his face. "I got here in—" He peered at the large watch on his skinny wrist. "In twenty-three minutes. I would have gotten here sooner, but I had to stop for construction." He extended a sweaty hand. "I'm Rene Torres."

Marisa shook his hand, which appeared to have just enough strength to lift pencils and pens but nothing heavier. She was mystified. She had shaken hands with adults but never with someone her own age, and it felt strange.

"It's a pleasure to meet you," he said, his head bowing slightly.

She gawked at him. This guy didn't talk like a kid. She sensed that her mouth hung open, but she couldn't help herself.

"How was your day?" Rene asked.

How was my day? she thought. *This boy is* muy *wimpy.* Still, she answered without a hint of sarcasm, "Okay, I guess," and quickly added, "How come you're tutoring Roberto?" If he was going to try to make conversation, she might as well do her part.

"Because he needs help," Rene explained. "I like it and I get paid. He plans to go into ROTC in college and then into the army, but he needs to retool the mechanical side of his brain."

"Roberto has a brain?" Marisa almost blurted out. Instead, she asked, "How come you were hanging with him?"

"He was going to give me a ride to Office Depot."

More pens for this guy's shirt pocket, she thought snidely. She caught herself being mean and didn't like it.

Rene stuffed his handkerchief into his front pocket. He shifted his gaze from her face to the front of the school. Two boys were digging their hands into a bag of potato chips. A girl on her cell phone was yelling, "You lyin', girl! You snatched it without paying a damn dime!" Sneaking a quick smoke, a janitor had his hands cupped around a cigarette.

Marisa could tell that the nerd wasn't familiar with her kind of school, one with security guards who themselves looked like thugs. She felt a little embarrassed at the yellow lawn, the torn blinds in the front window, and the steps splattered with old gum. The American flag was hoisted only halfway—due to a problem with the broken chain that hauled it up—and gave the impression that the school was in mourning. Someone or something had died, perhaps something called hope.

"Roberto wants to be an army officer?" Marisa asked. If he was such a good guy, why did he cheat on Alicia? She would have thrown out the question but heard someone shriek from the front steps, "Who's that? Einstein?" A crew of girls bent over holding their sides laughing.

"Come down here and say that! We can chunk right here!" Marisa barked. Her hands curled into fists and then uncurled, each of her long fingernails like daggers.

None of the girls moved, but none stopped laughing. They guffawed and did a dance around the backpacks at their feet.

"My school is sick," Marisa grumbled. "I wish I went to a different one." There, it was out. She had thought it often but never said it.

"Don't worry about me," Rene said. "People are always picking on me."

Marisa winced at his admission. "They wouldn't pick on you if I was around. They would show you some respect." She was surprised by her proclamation. She hadn't known the nerd more than five minutes and yet she was defending him. She could tell that he was shorter than she by an inch or two, and certainly a lot skinnier. The buckle was on his belt's last hole.

Rene was touched. "That's very nice of you."

"Come on." Marisa beckoned. She was curious about Rene. He was so different from the homeboys she knew.

Rene turned his bike around and walked it down the street, where potato chip bags, smashed paper cups and hamburger wrappers scuttled in the wind Cars passed with radios blaring and the drivers shouting over the songs. Marisa led Rene to a small park, where they sat on the grass. A woman bundled up in three sweaters was feeding pigeons. A sea of pigeons the color of cement followed her as she tossed seeds to the left, then the right.

"Here, before I forget." Rene brought out her cell phone from his fanny pack. "You got a couple of calls, but I didn't answer them. I believe strongly in privacy. That's why I'm so against the policies of our country. Privacy is becoming scarce."

What's he talking about? Marisa wondered. *Does he always talk like this?*

"Like right now, we assume we have privacy, but if the Secret Service wanted they could listen to our conversation."

"We ain't said anything," Marisa argued. It was usually she who was the chatterbox, but she found herself growing quiet. A leaf floated down from the maple tree and settled on her knee. She flicked the leaf from her knee, stood up, and brought Rene's cell phone from her pocket. "What's so important about privacy, anyhow? My mom doesn't give me privacy. She'll come in and check my drawers to see if I have drugs and stuff."

Rene looked disbelieving. He licked his lips, assembled some nerve by puffing up his muscle-depleted chest, and started to ask, "You don't do..."

"*¡Chale!* I don't do drugs. All I'm saying is..." She thought, *What am I saying? Why are we talking about stupid stuff?* Suddenly her anger began to cook inside her, but was that heated cauldron going to spill onto a boy who wore white socks and carried a handkerchief? He didn't deserve it.

Another leaf floated downward in a seesaw motion and settled on Rene's bony kneecap. Rene took the leaf between his thumb and index finger and twirled it. "It's the end of life for this leaf."

Marisa seized the leaf from Rene and was about to crumple it when she was struck by the cruelty of her thoughts. *He's so skinny, skinnier than Roberto. He should eat more. Work out with weights. Man, this guy's a genuine nerd.*

"You think I should go?" Rene stood up and leaned over to pick up his bicycle.

Another leaf slowly descended from the tree and hooked itself in Rene's curly hair.

"You're kinda silly, you know," Marisa remarked. Her anger had disappeared and so had her brooding thoughts. She had had a hard day at school—a C on a math quiz, and a C minus that was almost a D on a history exam. She had figured that this was the source of her grumpiness and that it had nothing to do with the boy sitting next to her.

"I would describe myself as occasionally preposterous, but never silly," he countered. "I know people laugh at me...Are you laughing at me?"

"No way!" Marisa crowed.

"It's okay if you are."

"I'm straight-up. I ain't laughing!"

The woman with the pigeon feed passed them with the pigeons parading behind.

They twirled leaves and Marisa, pulling her hair back behind her ears, scooted a little closer to him. She would later debate with herself what that little gesture meant. But for now she was enjoying the presence of this boy, whose bicycle was too big for him and whose eyeglasses were crooked on his cute small face.

That night her father wolfed down his dinner—a second evening of *albóndigas,* but this time with a salad drenched with bottled blue cheese dressing—and hurried out the front door with his bowling ball. It was Wednesday, when he played in a thirty-five-and-older league. There was a whistle on his lips.

"Mom," Marisa said after she had done the dishes and returned to the living room wiping her hands on a dish towel. She could tell that her mother was in a good mood, because she was listening to her favorite CD: Linda Ronstadt's *Canciones de mi Padre.*

"What?" her mother asked. She was seated on the couch with a blanket over her knees, reading an old *People* magazine.

"Mom, I want to go to a new school." She had made this decision when she watched Rene ride away in an awkward crooked path. He had no leg strength, no way to protect himself. True, she had Alicia to protect, but Rene really needed help or he might be squashed like a bug.

"Did you see Ricky Martin's mansion? He's got seven bathrooms." Her mother's eyes were lit with excitement. "I wish we had two bathrooms. That wouldn't be asking too much."

"Mom, I don't like my school."

Her mother turned a page of the magazine and whistled at the sight of a blue pool overlooking the sea. "I wish he would invite me over for a barbecue and a swim." She licked a finger and turned another page.

"My grades aren't so great and I was thinking that if I used Aunt Sara's address, I could go to Hamilton. I could get a transfer." She pointed northward, where Hamilton Magnet High School was located among nice homes. "It's a much better school."

Her mother put down her magazine and sat up. Ricky Martin's seven bathrooms went down the toilet in a large surge. "What are you saying?"

"About going to a new high school. I hate mine. Everyone's into drugs and stuff. There's this freshman girl named Jasmine who even got pregnant."

"And you?" The question was calm, yet serious. Her mother sat up straight with the magazine on her lap.

"Nah, Mom," she replied. Although she could see Ricky Martin's perfect smile on the cover of the magazine, Marisa couldn't share in his happiness for his seven bathrooms or the pool that could probably fit all of her ninth-grade class. His smile seemed completely fake.

"Then why?"

"I don't know. Maybe I could do better." Marisa imagined herself sitting up in class and really listening to her English teacher. She could see Rene in the corner, his hand up, because he was the one with the mouthful of answers.

"How are you going to get to that school from here?"

Marisa was prepared. "You can take me when you go to work."

Her mother worked part-time as a receptionist at a real estate office. It was a job that required her to spend her hours in front of the photocopy machine. She was the one who cradled a phone receiver in her neck and greeted, "Green River Realty. How may I help you?"

Her mother's gaze wandered over the soft landscape of Marisa's young face, searching for clues of mischief.

"I don't understand you," her mother tried.

"There's nothing to understand, Mom. We can use Auntie Sara's address to get a transfer. Our drinking fountains don't work and almost none of the toilets flush." Marisa was shivering slightly, though the living room was anything but cold. It was the shiver of something close to fear, yet not fear.

"Are you in trouble at school?" her mother asked.

"No, Mom, there ain't no drama."

"Is it because of Roberto?"

"Hecka no," she told her mother, bristling at the mention of his name.

"Then what, *mi'ja*?"

She sat next to her mother but didn't unbutton her heart. She squeezed her mother's hand. "Please. You'll see. I need to go to a better school."

Marisa's mother brushed her daughter's hair with her fingers. "We want you to do good in life."

"I want to do good, too. What do you think?" Marisa asked with a begging quiver in her voice.

"I think we can give your *tía* a call," her mother finally said.

Marisa hugged her mother, crushing the face of Ricky Martin in the magazine. "You're the best, Mom!"

Marisa was going to explain to her mother her strategy about becoming a better student when she heard her cell phone ring in the bedroom. She found herself jumping up and running to get it, hoping to answer before her abrupt recorded message came on.

"Hey," she greeted.

"This is Rene."

"Rene who?" Marisa asked roughly. Her front teeth bit her lower lip. She'd sounded cruel. "Oh, god, I'm sorry for sounding so, so..."

"So forthright," Rene completed for her.

"So what?"

"Oh, you know, direct and honest." Rene giggled and jokingly announced, "I'm looking for new students for my tutoring business. You want to hire me? It's two lessons for the price of one this week."

Marisa pictured the two of them hunkered together over a large math textbook.

"You think I'm dumb, huh?"

"No," Rene protested. "I just wanted to call."

"Oh," she mumbled.

Silence.

"Are you done with your homework?" Rene finally said.

Done? She hadn't even pulled it out of her backpack and wasn't sure if she would bother since she was going to start a new school.

"Oh yeah, it's almost done," she lied. She was nervous, aware that this was the first time she had ever got a call from a boy. She nibbled on her hair, spat it out, and blurted, "Guess what school I'm transferring to?"

Chapter

Hamilton Magnet High School was located far up north where the Sierras peeked through the valley smog. Marisa was unfamiliar with her new school, though she suspected that most of the students came from homes where money grew on trees. But she had to admit that she might be wrong. Maybe those money trees were bare and fruitless, and maybe the students had their own fears.

What was certain about Hamilton Magnet? Every fall when Washington played Hamilton in football, her former high school crushed them under their grinding cleats. Her new school was also smaller—nine hundred students—and whiter. Washington was mostly Latinos and blacks, with whites and Asians who acted Latino and black. The shaved-headed Asians with bluish skulls would holler in the hallways, arms flailing, "*Chale, sapo,* I can't lend you *mi ranfla* for the party. *Mi jefita* took *mis llaves.*"

The transfer took only three days—one day to convince her father and two for her high school to do the paperwork for the transfer—by which time Alicia was out of the hospital. Now Alicia was home in bed with get-well balloons that floated to the bedroom ceiling but in time would sink down to the floor. There was a problem between the friends. Alicia had found out about her fight with Roberto at the hospital. Marisa couldn't believe Alicia was mad about that. Didn't she realize Marisa had been defending her?

"Please call," Marisa had whined. But Alicia didn't call.

Marisa's aunt Sara was happy about the transfer—she lived only three blocks away from Hamilton Magnet and looked forward to her favorite niece staying over some nights. Her aunt was a nurse and wanted to encourage Marisa toward this profession. Marisa, out of respect, could only nod when she spoke to her aunt on the telephone and respond lamely, "Sounds fun, *Tía.* Sounds like you can make a lot of money." In truth, Marisa was leery of hospitals. Isn't that where you went when you were hurt or ready to die? Or to get in a fight? She had only to think of that two-faced Roberto. Then she remembered Rene. Maybe that's where you can meet—she gulped at this—a boy.

The first morning at her new school, Marisa maneuvered herself down the hallway, searching for Rene. She was nervous and on any other day would have snarled when a boy bumped her backpack. But this new school was unfamiliar territory, not the place to holler "Watch where you're going, *pendejo*!"

She spied Rene tying his shoes in the courtyard. She made a face at the white socks—she would have to talk to him about those socks and the high-water pants. She would have to tell him that he had to dress with the times.

"Hi Rene," she said as she approached him. Her voice, she sensed, was flat. She had been happy to get Rene's call three nights ago, but now was different.

He stood up, waving an arm bearing an oversized watch.

"It's good to see you, Marisa," Rene said brightly "How do you like it here?"

"I guess it's okay. But I don't know anybody except you."

"Nine hundred students." He gave a honking laugh and said, "Nine hundred and one students now"

"Rene, are you being funny?"

He nodded and honked his laughter again.

Marisa scanned the school yard She told him that she had an appointment with a counselor before classes.

"Hope you get Mr. Laird. He's real nice."

Marisa noticed his pants cuff caught in his sock. "Oh, god," she moaned, but admonished herself for thinking of the N-word—*nerd*

"Rene, we're going to have to talk," Marisa remarked as she nudged him away "But first, I'm hungry." Her eye had caught sight of a snack bar with a fluttering neon light.

"Talk about what?" He produced a cleanly folded handkerchief from his pocket and began to clean his eyeglasses. His eyes were beady as a salamander's.

"Stuff," she answered vaguely, aware that the time wasn't right. She prodded him toward the snack bar, where she eyed the doughnuts and the array of pies, apple being her favorite though chocolate was way up there, too. Her gaze floated up to the bananas speckled with dark spots. She debated whether to enjoy a true sugar rush or the much healthier banana. Last night, while eating a bowl of ice cream—her last, she'd promised—she had decided to stay away from cookies, ice cream, sodas, and potato chips. She was determined to shed a few pounds.

"Give me...," she said to the student behind the screen window. "Give me an apple—no, no, a banana." She turned to Rene. "You gonna get anything?"

He wagged his head no. His eyeglasses were crooked on his face.

"That's sixty cents," the girl said through the screen.

Marisa let six dimes roll from her palm and slapped one before it fell off the counter.

The two sat on a bench away from the milling crowd. She peeled back her banana and offered a bite to Rene

"No, I had some in my Wheaties," he said.

Marisa laughed and nearly dropped the banana. She was thinking, *He eats Wheaties? The "breakfast of champions"? Then how come he's so...*weak*?* But she admonished herself for the second time within ten minutes. She was no better than he, a fourteen-year-old girl with her own problems. She didn't want to be stuck-up.

"What's funny?" Rene asked.

"Nothing's funny," Marisa finally answered after clearing her throat of the first bite of overripe and mushy banana. "It's just kind of weird being here."

"You'll like it," Rene said. "I'm glad you're here. There's lots to do."

"What do you mean?"

"Like clubs."

"You belong to a club?" Marisa had never belonged to anything except Girl Scouts for a month. She would have stayed longer except she had eaten six boxes of Girl Scout Cookies and didn't have the means to pay for them—the thin mints were irresistible.

"Yeah, I belong to the science club."

Marisa stuffed the banana in her mouth to keep from laughing.

"And chess team. Plus thespians. Though I have never been in a play. But I like to read them in bed. I used to be able to recite some of *Hamlet.* 'To be, or not to be—that is the question; / Whether 'tis nobler in the mind to suffer / The slings . . .' I learned it when I was in sixth grade."

Marisa let the banana stay in her mouth. Her stomach was convulsing with laughter.

"Are you okay?" Rene asked as he jumped to his feet. "I know the Heimlich maneuver." He moved behind the bench and embarrassed Marisa, who couldn't help but think, *He's so cute. He's trying to save my life!*

Then there came a shout from one of four girls passing by. "Is that your girlfriend?"

Marisa broke out of Rene's grip. She had already swallowed the mouthful of banana and her mind was assembling words to throw like daggers at the girl who had taunted her—no, taunted Rene. But she thought better of the situation. This was her first day. Plus, she had promised herself not to get so angry.

"Are you better now?" Rene asked. "I took a first aid class at the YMCA and know quite a bit about saving people." He said this with his arm hooked in hers.

Marisa met with Mr. Laird, a counselor, who sat behind a paper-cluttered desk pulverizing one breath mint after another as he examined her transfer papers. He offered a mint to Marisa, who declined.

"Your test scores are good," he reported as he closed her file. "But your grades from your last school..." He sighed and tapped his pencil against her file.

"I know," she agreed. She had been examining some of his awards on the wall behind him, but now her attention was leveled at him. "But I'm going to do better here."

"I want you to," he remarked.

"I want to, too." She was serious.

"Good," he said, and stood up, pulling a sweater off a hat rack. He walked her to her American history class and said, "Let's have lunch together later."

Marisa was baffled. *Lunch? With an adult?* But she accepted his offer and held her breath as she entered her new class.

American history was not unlike history class at her old school, except most of the students were listening. When the bell rang, Mrs. Webb called Marisa to stay behind.

"Did I do something?" Marisa asked as she approached the teacher's desk.

"No," Mrs. Webb said with a kind radiance in her eyes. "I just want to welcome you to our school. If you have any questions about the material, please see me." Mrs. Webb pulled a book from a shelf, wrote the identification number in her roll book, and handed the heavy tome to Marisa. She informed her that they were on chapter four.

"Thank you," Marisa said in a near whisper.

Mrs. Webb patted Marisa's shoulder. "I'm so glad you're here."

By third period Marisa had learned the names of some of her classmates. She had thought she would be treated like an outsider, a *chola* girl with brown lipstick. But she was wrong; she was glad to be wrong. At lunch she found Rene sitting in the cafeteria, where they had agreed to meet.

"I bought you milk," Rene said. "It's chocolate. You like chocolate, don't you?"

"Rene, are you trying to spoil me?" She could chug chocolate milk all day. "I was in such a rush that I forgot my lunch."

"I could share mine. And if I wanted to spoil you, I would have bought you two chocolates." He laughed like someone in the fit of an asthmatic attack.

They went outside to sit on the grass and drink their cartons of milk. Rene offered her one of his two peanut-butter-and-jelly sandwiches. Marisa took the sandwich from him while staring at his white socks. She debated whether she should tell him or just shut her big mouth. She almost got the nerve to pull off his shoes and strip him of those socks.

In the end she decided to stuff her mouth with a large bite of sandwich and to say nothing. Rene brought out a Ziploc bag full of animal crackers. She took a hippopotamus and nibbled at its stubby feet.

"You want to try out for the play?" Rene asked. He was eating an elephant animal cracker.

"What play?" The entire hippo was settled on her back molars. Her tongue began to work it loose.

"Romeo and Juliet."

She almost spat out the cookie.

"You're joking?" Marisa asked.

"No, I'm not. Auditions are this week."

"I never been in no play." Marisa chuckled. She fit another animal cookie into her mouth and asked, "What, am I going to try to be Juliet? In case you haven't noticed..." Without hesitation, she pinched at a layer of fat.

"You don't have to try out for her—" Here he stopped. "You can try out for the nurse."

"Who's the nurse?"

Rene plucked a handful of grass and tossed it into the air. "It's a real meaty part—you'll have to learn lots of lines, but I can help."

Marisa was touched and caught some of the grass as it came down. She slapped the grass from her palms and scratched her nose.

"Or there's a musician." Rene raised his arms and pretended to be playing a violin.

"Do you play violin?" she asked.

"I used to. Now I'm concentrating on piano. And I have a recorder, but I hardly ever practice."

She scooted closer to him. She peeled a crumb of animal cracker from his cheek and wondered why she felt so comfortable with a boy she hardly knew.

Rene took her hand. His thumb rubbed her thumb.

"A penny for your thoughts," he said.

She was thinking: *A boy had never called me before. A boy is feeding me cookies on a damp lawn. A boy is wearing white socks and I refuse to call him a nerd or anything mean. What's going on with me?*

"Yeah," she answered, and would have followed her simple *yeah* with more explanation except she caught sight of Mr. Laird, the counselor, walking toward them.

"Dang," she muttered. "I forgot I was supposed to have lunch with him."

Rene released Marisa's hand. He stood up, swiping at the grass on the back of his pants, and announced, "Sir, I have good news."

The good news was that Marisa and Rene were going to audition for parts in *Romeo and Juliet.* She lay in bed that night, glowing with happiness. She had the urge to call Alicia and tell her about Rene, but she held back because of Roberto—Alicia, heartbroken and now saddled with crutches, was hurting in a big way. Plus, Alicia was still acting mad at her. Was it because Marisa had knocked her boyfriend around? Or was she upset—or was it sad?—that she had moved to a new school?

"I'm going to lose weight," she muttered. "I really, really, really mean it." For dinner she had no second helpings and only two dinky scoops of ice cream, though she savored the flavor by keeping the spoon in her mouth like a thermometer.

"We're like Romeo and Juliet," she told herself with a chuckle. She pressed a pillow into her face and through the darkness could see Rene with his white socks and his bent eyeglasses on his cute face. She could help him change, and—*Yeah, I know,* she thought—he could also help her change.

Chapter

During her first few days at Hamilton Magnet, Marisa felt like she was on audition among her classmates. They kept looking at her—the new girl with brown lipstick and teased hair—and some would smile and others would just stare at her with flat, uninterested eyes. A few of the Latinos gave her looks that said, "I know you, girl," and she would return the stare at them until they turned away. Her chewing gum—Juicy Fruit, her favorite—would snap like a whip when one of them stared too long. Mean thoughts surfaced like a shark. If anybody had looked at her like that at her old school, she'd have slapped them.

But she struggled to remain cool

"It's different," she told her mother one morning as they drove up north through the suburbs.

"What do you mean?" she asked.

"It's so... white." She then asked, "Mom, you ever eat tofu?"

"*Eat?* Isn't tofu a martial art?"

"Nah, Mom, it's some kind of food. They serve it at school."

Later Marisa learned that tofu was a soy product, which she tasted in a veggie burger. Her tongue registered a simple description: *tasty.* She also learned that Rene was a vegetarian and avoided most milk products, though he would chug his favorite chocolate milk when he could.

"Milk isn't good for you," he announced. "At least the way the dairies keep cows. Most dairies are really filthy."

"What are you talking about? Like Milk Duds aren't good for you?" Marisa refused to believe that Milk Duds were unhealthy.

Rene nearly doubled over in asthmatic laughter. Finally he said, "No, Milk Duds aren't good for you, but I like them." After he controlled his laughter, he remarked, "And I like you."

"Get out of here, homeboy." Marisa was suddenly shy as a pony.

"But I do. Right now I'm missing a chess club meeting because of you."

Marisa was touched. "You're missing chess club for me? That's so sweet."

He pulled on her arm saying, "Come on."

They headed for the gym, where boys were playing basketball in street clothes—their pants precariously low on their hips. They hurried through the gym, where their classmates cast momentary glances at them, then dropped their interest immediately.

"Where we going?" Marisa asked as they walked quickly down a hallway.

"You'll see."

Soon Marisa stood in a darkened room where ancient weights lay dusty and forgotten. The boxing bag was deflated, and the wrestling mat was cracked. Football helmets lay like skulls against the wall

"They don't use this part of the gym anymore," Rene explained.

"Then what are we doing here?" Marisa asked. She wondered if Rene had brought her there to wrap his skinny arms around her thick middle, and possibly bury his face into her neck. But she was wrong about his intentions. Rene wanted to exercise his masculinity in a different way

He lay on a bench, spit into his palms, and said, "Pile it on."

"Get out of here!"

"Come on, Marisa," he begged. "I want to get strong. I wouldn't lift weights in the presence of anyone but you."

He's so cute, she thought tenderly. She handed him a bar with weights on each end. He accepted the burden with a grunt.

"It's heavy. What do we have here—fifty pounds?"

Marisa didn't have the heart to tell him that he was lifting the equivalent of two soup cans tied on the ends of a broomstick.

"It's dark in here. I can't read the numbers. But, yeah, it's about fifty pounds, maybe more."

He did a set of ten lifts, got up smacking his hands, and announced, "I want to get me swolles, some muscle."

Marisa picked up the pen that had rolled from his shirt pocket.

"Every day I want to come here and pump iron!" Rene flexed his left, then right, biceps. "I want to be like the Terminator."

"If you want me to help you, then give me a kiss." Marisa couldn't believe she had said that!

His arms became as limp as wet noodles. "A kiss?" he asked weakly as he lowered his head. He gazed down at the weights on the ground. "How about one more set first?"

He did two more sets, grunting through clenched teeth. They returned to the main quad of the campus just as the bell began to ring. Lunchtime was over, along with Marisa's opportunity to push her boy against the wall and force a kiss out of him. But she did blurt out, "Rene, you got to do something about your socks."

"They're clean."

"Nah, homeboy, your clothes ain't tight." She felt pity for the guy. "You can't wear white socks like you do."

Rene peeked at the lower extremities of his high-water pants.

"Your socks gotta match your pants."

"My mom never says anything." He offered his baffled face to her.

Marisa propped her hands on her hips and wiggled her bottom. "Big boy, do I look like your mama?"

Rene smiled as he tugged on his pants legs, trying to hide the blazing whiteness of his socks. "No, you look like..." He began his asthmatic laughter. "You look—*honk*—like—*honk*—my—*honk, honk*—my hot mama!"

They put their first kiss on hold.

It was early evening when Alicia called.

"Marisa, it's me."

Marisa closed her bedroom door to block out the sound of the mixer going at high speed in the kitchen. "What's going on?"

Silence.

"Are you mad at me?" Marisa asked.

Alicia didn't answer the question. "How come you're at that new school? You think you're better than us?" Her voice sounded forced and unnatural, as if she had been practicing the lines of a bad play and couldn't get them right.

"I never said I was better than you." Marisa was hurt. She raised a fingernail to her mouth and chewed.

"I didn't say that. Some other girl said that."

Marisa pictured her so-called friends cutting her up, calling her a coconut—brown on the outside but white at the core. They were probably calling her fat, tangle haired, smelly maybe, and extending their insults to her family.

"I don't care what other people think. They're stupid. I'm happier over there."

"How come you don't like it over here?"

"Here" was a school with no working drinking fountain, no nets on the basketball rims, no toilets that flushed consistently, no teachers who hadn't had their cars keyed or tires poked with ice picks. "Here" was a school whose flag could only be hoisted halfway up.

"I'll be straight-up and tell you I don't like Washington," Marisa stated firmly. "It's nasty. I just want to do something different." To change the subject, she asked Alicia how her leg was. She almost asked about Roberto.

"When am I going to see you?" Alicia asked. "I'm going crazy in my room."

Marisa felt for her friend. "Yeah, you're stuck in bed."

"Nah, it hurts a little bit, but I can get around."

They made plans to get together at a school car wash at Marisa's *old* school, Washington.

"Heard from Roberto?" Marisa risked asking.

"He left some messages on my machine, but I'm not calling him back."

"Right on, girl." Marisa told her friend that she had to go, that her mother was screaming for help in the kitchen.

"I miss you," Alicia murmured.

Marisa was confused. First Alicia had called to say that a bunch of shanky classmates were talking about her. Then she was being all friendly.

"I'll call you," she told Alicia.

In the kitchen her mother was licking the blades of the hand mixer.

"You want some?" her mother asked. She handed Marisa a whirly blade white with frosting. Marisa took the blade and made a swipe with her finger. As she licked the frosting she warned herself, "That's twenty calories and more if I keep going!" She set the blade into the sink. "What did you want, Mom?"

"I want you to finish the cake." Her mother pointed at a lopsided cake that required a layer of frosting. "Use a plastic spatula."

Marisa plastered the cake with frosting and then helped make *frijoles.* She oiled a pan, set it on a burner, and after a long minute scooped beans into it. The beans, little troopers, sizzled and marched in the pan.

"Mom, do you think I should be going to Hamilton instead of staying at Washington?" Marisa mashed the beans and added a handful of yellow cheese.

Wearing mismatched oven mitts, her mother slowly brought a pan of red enchiladas out of the oven and set it on the counter. "*Claro.* Of course you should." She took off the mitts and peeled back the aluminum foil. Steam rose against her face. "Why? Don't you like it there?"

"Yeah, I do, except I just got a call from Alicia."

"*Pobrecita.* How's her leg?"

"She's home and she's getting around on crutches." Marisa hesitated but finally informed her mother that some shisty girls were talking about her.

"So let those *cholas* talk about you like that!" Her mother was furious, like a blender on high. "Just because you're going to a better school. They're jealous!" She cupped her hands and yelled to the den, "Rafael! It's dinner."

"I like it at my new school," Marisa said.

"I know you do. You're going to do well." She cupped her hands and called out a second time, "Rafael—*ven!* We're waiting for you."

Marisa poured iced tea from a pitcher, and instead of doctoring hers with scoops of sugar, she took it plain. When she cut into her enchilada, steam rose and moistened her forehead. She blew on a forkful and told her father, "Dad, I'm trying out for a play."

"¿Cómo?" His big mustache went up and down as he chewed.

"I'm going out for *Romeo and Juliet.*"

He chewed and chewed, cleared his throat, wiped his mouth with his napkin, picked up a grain of *arroz* that had fallen from his fork onto the table, and remarked, "I used to know Romeo and Juliet."

"Dad, get out of here," Marisa said in disbelief.

"No, really," he said as one hand absently rubbed the front of his stomach. "Back in high school. There was a guy, Romeo Garcia, and his girlfriend was Julieta Mendoza. They were an item."

As she drank, Marisa stared at her father through the bottom of her glass of iced tea. Her father seldom veered far from the truth. She listened as he told her how Romeo loved his Julieta until this other guy came along.

"Who was this other dude?"

He looked her straight in his eye. "It was me."

Marisa's mother slapped his arm. "*Mentiroso.* You were too busy chopping cotton to have a girlfriend."

"Chopping cotton." He chuckled with both hands on the ball of his stomach. "That's how I met Julieta." He winked at his daughter and went for a second helping.

Marisa was in bed, near the edge of sleep with her math book in her face, when her cell phone rang. She rose up onto her elbows and plucked her phone from the headboard, where she kept her stuffed animals.

"Yeah?" she asked, face draped with her hair. She swept it out of her eyes, which were still closed but suddenly opened when the voice asked, "How's Alicia?"

Roberto—the rat, *la rata.*

"Why are you calling?" Marisa glared at the clock on her chest of drawers. The clock glowed *10:18.*

"I'm calling because Alicia won't answer her phone."

"She don't want to see you. You broke her leg. Worse, you cheated on her and Alicia told me that girl in the photo was *muy fea.*" She snapped closed her math book and set it roughly onto the floor.

Marisa could hear Roberto swallow. He muttered, "How come our school ain't good enough for you?"

She clicked off the phone as she muttered, "*Tonto* jerk." But a second later the phone rang again. She picked it up and roared a frosty, "I said she don't want to talk to you."

"You don't want to talk to me?"

It was Rene, a lamb with no sins except bad taste in clothes.

"Oh, Rene, it's you! I'm sorry." Marisa sat up and rubbed the hammer of her right fist against her sleepy eyes.

"I'm calling you because..."

"Because you like me?" Marisa risked. "You're so sweet."

"Yeah—" He giggled. "And because I got up to doing fifteen push-ups without stopping."

"My Terminator!" Marisa crowed.

"Oh, come on, Marisa, I'm not really that strong yet."

Marisa could see him bashfully lowering his face. She pictured him doing each of the fifteen push-ups and shaking from the pain as he touched his nose to the floor.

"Yes, you are!"

"Oh, my," Rene whispered and then told her that his mother had bought him a pack of blue socks.

Chapter

After school Marisa leafed through a worn copy of *Romeo and Juliet* and was smart enough to figure out that neither she nor Rene could play the leads, though she had a faint inkling that perhaps they could bring a new angle to those roles. After all, couldn't Juliet be fat and Romeo skinny? And weren't they in love?

They were straddling a bench under a tree that had given up all its leaves. The school campus was nearly empty. Somewhere a janitor was vacuuming a classroom. Somewhere kids were playing football on a brownish field.

"I could be a really, really skinny Romeo," Rene remarked. He handed Marisa a stick of gum.

"Then I'm Juliet." Marisa unwrapped the gum from its silvery foil and folded it into her mouth. "Thanks for the gum, Romeo." She turned her attention momentarily to a lone skateboarder riding halfway up a cement wall nicked with wheel skids.

"The gum is from my trick-or-treat candy."

Marisa shoved him. "Getta outta here! You didn't go trick-or-treating. Anyway, Halloween ain't for another week."

"It's from my last year's stash."

Marisa rolled the gum onto the carpet of her tongue and was ready to deposit it into her hand when Rene said, "Just kidding."

"What's your mother like?" Marisa asked.

"Tall and kind of strict." He chewed his gum loudly. "What's yours like?"

"Short and sometimes really angry about things." In truth, her mother had softened. She was glad about her daughter's new school, though Marisa had told her nothing about Rene. "What's your dad like?"

"Short," Rene answered. "But my parents are divorced." He looked into the distance as if his father was somewhere far away and he was trying to catch a glimpse of him. Marisa sighed and wished she hadn't asked the question. They laced their hands together and wiggled their fingers.

"What about the play?" Marisa asked. "I don't know any of these characters." She ran down the cast: Mercutio, Escalus, Benvolio, Nurse. Marisa tapped the word *nurse.*

"I'll play the nurse, like you said earlier. I could play a person helping other people."

"Marisa, it's not like a *nurse,* nurse. This character is sort of like... a babysitter."

Marisa wrinkled her forehead, confused.

"In the play, the nurse is Juliet's helper, you know, like someone who helps her dress and stuff. She's like a confidante."

"Where did you learn to talk like that?" Marisa asked. "I never use words like that one you said."

"The word is *confidante.* It means someone you tell your innermost thoughts to without worrying. What you tell that person is kept between you two."

"Oh, so if I tell you something really private, you'll keep it to yourself?"

"That's right." Rene tapped the toe of his shoe. "So what are you going to tell me?"

"I'm not going to tell you anything. You'll tell somebody in your chess club."

"I won't! I'm your confidant." He made a large swooping crossing motion across his heart. His Adam's apple rode up and down as he waited for her to deliver a secret. "So what is it?"

Right then the skateboarder rolled back, hands in his pockets, and taunted, "Hey, doofus!"

Marisa's fists clenched. "What did you say?" She pulled her leg over the bench like she was getting off a horse, ready to smack him one.

The skateboarder sailed away, shirttail flapping His greenish hair was like a horn on top of his head.

"He's a pimply *güey.*" Her chest was heaving. She was aware that her new classmates were sizing the two of them up, and earlier in the week she had heard snickers when they'd passed by together in the hallway. But this was the first direct verbal strike. *What is it to him, that ugly fool?*

"I don't care," Rene said. "So what's your secret?"

Marisa breathed in and out several times as she calmed herself. She assembled nice thoughts and, nervously turning the ring on her thumb, announced, "Well, Mr. Confidence, I have never had a *beso* laid on me."

"What?"

"A kiss, homeboy."

"You mean your grandmother never kissed you?"

"No, not like that! You know what I mean." She closed her eyes and waited for Rene to bring his face toward hers. She waited and waited, then peeked through the shadows of her eyelashes. Her eyes sprang open. Rene was no longer next to her

From the corner of her eye she could see the skateboarder who had taunted Rene. He was on his back, his legs fanning in and out, hurt by a spill. He meant nothing to her. "What are you doing?" she called to Rene, who was at a nearby trash can.

"Getting rid of my chewing gum," he hollered in return as he tried to shake the gum into the trash can. The gum was stuck to his fingers.

Oh, he's such a nerd, she thought, then closed her eyes and waited for him to return.

Rene tasted of Juicy Fruit when Marisa finally got her first *beso.*

The auditorium was dark and the students were half lit in the stage lights. Marisa's stomach turned nervously. She reviewed the students—one she recognized from her English class—and then the director who had his eyeglasses sitting on his forehead. His shirt cuffs were rolled up. His belly bounced when he took a long step, demonstrating an action.

"I don't know," Marisa said nervously. Her feet seemed to stick to the floor.

"Come on," Rene begged, and hooked his arm into hers.

They read for parts, and they were assigned to be in the chorus. The director, Mr. Mitchell, soothed them by saying they were stupendous actors but singing voices were also needed.

"But I can't sing," Marisa whined to Rene.

"You can try whisper-singing," Rene suggested. "And there's so many of us that if we sound really bad no one will notice." He took Marisa's hand into his. "You were great up there. They should have given you a speaking part."

"Get out of here!" Giggling, Marisa unlaced her fingers from his hand. "I was terrible and you know it!" She had been asked to read lines—she was playing Juliet's mother—and she fumbled the ancient words, finally slapping the book against her thigh and saying to the drama coach, "People don't talk like this!" Holding her book up to her face to hide her embarrassed laughter, Marisa moved stage left while the director countered, "Oh, no, you did very, very well."

"No, really, we can practice singing. I'm going to practice in the shower." Rene then asked, "So how did I carry myself?"

So how did I carry myself? she pondered. For a moment Marisa assumed that he was quoting Shakespeare because he sounded—what was that word?—*theatrical*. He sounded English.

"What do you mean?"

"In my audition!"

Rene had read the part of Mercutio.

"You were tight."

"I was tight? I was that good?" Rene beamed and scratched his knee absently. "I have something to confess, Marisa."

Marisa snuggled up to him. "What, buddy boy?" She could smell his breath flavored with chewing gum.

"Well, you may not believe this, but I'm not really what you think I am." He flirted by blinking his eyelashes.

"What?" Marisa wanted to know everything about her first boyfriend, to delve into his secrets. He was gangly and smart, and had an odd laugh. But what wheels turned inside his head?

"I'm not really a nerd."

Marisa covered her mouth with her hand, laughing. She slapped his shoulder. "Yeah, you are."

"No, really! I'm very Shakespearean, very manly!"

Marisa laughed. Rene bent over and, through the fingers covering his mouth, honked out a funny ducklike laugh.

But Marisa was convinced that he was a nerd when he rode his bike to the car wash sponsored by her old high school that weekend. It was midmorning and the car wash was going poorly—only three cars had been washed and vacuumed. And the principal's car, a large Buick, was nasty with fingerprints all over the window and the ashtray filled with cigarette butts. He hadn't bothered to clean it up even a little bit.

Rene was holding his hand over his nose as he rode up.

"What happened?" Marisa first thought that he was going to pull his hand away from his face and reveal a fake nose and possibly a set of vampire teeth. But when he did she saw a rivulet of blood.

"I fell off my bike," he explained as he rolled his bicycle toward the chain-link fence near the tennis courts.

"Someone jumped you, huh?" She scanned the street.

One of the girls from Washington approached them. "Who's he?"

Without answering, Marisa led Rene to the curb, where he sat, head back, the blood staining his throat. A coin of blood fell and splashed onto his wrist.

"How did it happen?" she asked again, this time sternly.

Rene shrugged.

Marisa had got into fights and had won some and lost others—one of the losses showed in a faint jagged scar under her chin, which at night in bed she would trace with her finger. She'd bloodied noses and had her own nose blossom with blood from roundhouse punches. It didn't matter to her—life, as she had discovered so far, was mostly knocks and punches. But she felt rudely offended that her boyfriend—he *was* her boyfriend, wasn't he?—would be smacked around. He was so sweet. Who would hurt him?

Right then Roberto showed up, driving his parents' car. Marisa watched him emerge from the car, hugging friends and giving peace signs to those who were too cool to step forward. He jumped when someone sprayed him with the hose.

"Wait here," she instructed Rene. She got up and approached Roberto.

"Hey, girl," Roberto greeted.

"Hey yourself. She's not here."

Roberto slammed the car door.

"Who?" he asked, owl-like.

"You know who." She stared at him until he looked over her shoulder and sneered at Rene, who was standing up. "I'm going to have to smack that swanson again," he said.

Marisa bristled. "So it was you who hurt Rene?"

Roberto gave a ratlike smile. "Ah, I was just playing with him."

"You mean like this?" Marisa hauled off a punch to his shaved temple and a second punch that brought a flow of blood from his mouth. Even though he was an eleventh grader, Roberto wasn't that big—a little taller than she—and she had arm wrestled him before and knew what he could do.

"I don't want to hurt you!" He backed up, holding his lip. "You're a girl."

Some girls, wet from being sprayed with the hose by boys, pulled Marisa away.

"I had to do it because he didn't want to tutor me no more."

"You're hella freaky! So what!"

He backpedaled when Marisa, like a bull, started toward him. He shoved her with a straight arm and struck her in the face with the heel of his palm.

"You ain't gonna hurt me!" she bellowed. But she sensed by the taste of blood that he had cut her lip.

More girls pulled Marisa away, a loop of blood flying from her face. She stood breathing hard and hands shaking from the rush of adrenaline. By then Rene was at her side, pulling on her arm and begging, "Come on—let's go." To Roberto he yelled, "You better not hit her again."

They left the high school car wash, walking up the street, both feeling their injuries.

"He's the swanson, not you," Marisa growled. "My ex-school's stupid. You should have seen the principal's car—nasty!"

"Violence doesn't get you anywhere," Rene commented.

Marisa mumbled for him to be quiet.

"If he touches you like that again, I'm going to hit him back," Rene blubbered.

"You just said you're against violence."

"That's because I usually get beat up. But I don't care anymore."

Marisa hooked her arm in his. "We're messed up. Your nose is all red."

They continued down the street, kicking through the fall leaves. Rene stopped and patted the bar of his bicycle. "Get on."

Marisa hopped onto the bar and Rene straddled the bike, gripping the handlebars tightly. He kicked off, straining as he tried to pick up speed. He was pedaling for his girl, and Marisa was touched by his courage. With the two of them, the bicycle could crash to the asphalt street and rough them up even more. Could they stand two embarrassments in a span of ten minutes?

Chapter

Marisa fabricated a story of how she had hit her face on the shower nozzle—her uncle Pedro, a small man no taller than a boy, had done the remodeling on the bathroom several years before and assumed everyone was his height. The nozzle was positioned low.

Marisa vowed to stop fighting. She would stand by her nerdy boyfriend and learn to play chess, Rene's favorite pastime. She would come clean about her new life and learn chess in the presence of her mother and father. Rene, only slightly scared of meeting her parents, biked over on Sunday afternoon with the chessboard and pieces rattling in his backpack.

Marisa's mother had been ready to go shopping

when she opened the door to a young man who, she would later tell Marisa, resembled a clean-cut, young religious type going door-to-door handing out pamphlets.

"Mrs. Rodriguez, I'm Rene Torres, a classmate of Marisa's." He extended a hand and asked permission to leave his bike on the porch.

"Of course," she remarked without looking at the bike leaning on the rail. She let Rene pass, holding the door open for him. "Who is this skinny boy?" her face was asking. Marisa's father muted the television just as the Raiders, down three points, were attempting a forty-eight-yard field goal. He stood up to shake hands with Rene.

"Don't let us disturb you, sir," Rene said. "We're going to play chess."

Her father and mother gawked. Was this boy here to court their daughter? Why did the boy have a red nose? Did it have anything to do with their daughter's cut lip?

"Mom!" Marisa called, embarrassed by her mother's jaw hanging open.

"What?" she asked.

"You're staring."

Her mother's gawk reshaped itself into a smile. "I guess I am." Her mother clipped away into the kitchen, where, Marisa figured, she was leaning against the sink and pondering the meaning of a boy showing up at their door.

They played on the table in the den. Marisa's mother brought them cookies and milk, and her father, hiking up his pants, would enter the den periodically to report on the score between the Raiders and the Broncos.

"I can't believe my dad," Marisa muttered. Her father had left the television muted so that he could hear them—he'd given up his Sunday football to eavesdrop. Marisa could make out her mother tiptoeing from room to room—she, too, was trying to listen.

"They're concerned for your safety," Rene said. He moved a bishop and took a pawn from Marisa. "I might maul you any second."

Marisa wagged her head. "No way, homeboy."

"That was the first fight in my entire life." Rene moved his queen. "How did I do?"

"That wasn't your first fight—you lie!" Marisa exclaimed. She remembered fighting in kindergarten, when she had had an argument over a red crayon. "You must have had another one."

"I explained I'm against violence. And why's that, you might ask?"

Marisa remembered very clearly. "Because you

usually get beat up." Her hand crept over Rene's like a tarantula. She told him that her parents were funny, the way they were worrying about her. She giggled and moved her bishop two spaces.

"I wouldn't do that if I were you."

"I can do what I want. This is my house."

Rene slid his rook six spaces and took her queen. Marisa surveyed her lost pieces. Then she counted the pieces she had taken: one pawn. Even with Rene coaching her on her moves, she was headed to defeat. "I'm better at Candy Land."

"Candy Land!"

"I would slaughter you, buddy boy." Her smile hurt her cut lip and forced her to emit a faint "Ouch."

"Does it hurt a lot?" Rene asked.

"Only when you say something silly. And how's your nose?"

"Sore," he answered. Rene pushed Marisa's pieces back to her side and said, "Let's play again."

They played six games, and each one got easier for Marisa, who suspected that Rene was losing his pieces on purpose.

They were going to start a seventh game when Marisa's father stepped into the den, smiling. "Raiders won in overtime, 21–19." He hiked up his pants and asked, "Who's winning here?" Her mother then appeared from behind her father, "You want to stay for dinner? I'm defrosting some tamales."

"That's very nice," Rene replied. "But my mom expects me home for dinner."

Marisa turned and saw that it was still daylight Sunlight spilled in from the window.

"What's your last name again, Rene?" her father asked.

"Torres."

He pinched his chin. "Torres, Torres. I used to know a Manuel Torres from high school. Is that your father?"

"No, he's Ben Torres."

Marisa's father lowered his head and had the appearance of someone thinking deeply on a game show. "No, I don't know any Ben Torres."

"I know a Rebecca Torres," her mother cut in. She had brushed her hair and reddened her mouth with lipstick.

Marisa thought, *This is enough! We got to bounce out of here.* "We're going to go for a walk," she said.

Rene looked puzzled.

Marisa raked the chess pieces into his backpack and fit the board in carefully—she peeked in and noticed a dog-eared copy of *Romeo and Juliet.*

"Don't be long," Marisa's mother sang sweetly.

The two stood on the porch. Although sunlight still flickered off what leaves remained on the sycamore tree in the yard, Marisa shivered from the cold. But she hesitated over going back inside. Her parents would press her against the wall and begin to interrogate her. Just who was this *chavalo*?

Rene rolled his bike off the porch and Marisa jumped down the stairs. She was sure that her parents were peeking from the front window—she turned and caught sight of them ducking behind the curtains.

"They're nice," Rene said.

Marisa said nothing.

"You get on." She took the bike from Rene's grip.

"Me?" He stabbed a finger at his chest.

"Yes, you!"

When Rene hopped onto the bar, the bike nearly tipped over. But Marisa gripped the handlebars, kicked a leg over the seat, and pushed off, wobbly at first, then straightening and picking up speed as their shadow pursued them along the black asphalt.

"My, you're strong," Rene said.

Marisa had to laugh inside: *My, you're strong.* She had a boyfriend, and so what if he was a nerd?

They rode to the public playground, which was gated closed on Sunday, and sat on the grass.

"Watch this." Rene got into push-up position and did twenty-five shaky push-ups.

"You're gonna have some serious swolles in a month." She clapped her hands and pulled off a piece of grass stuck to his chin.

"I liked your parents," Rene said after he caught his breath. "They seemed so compatible."

Marisa didn't want to discuss her parents. No, she wanted to hear about his secrets—anything!

"I have no secrets. I'm an open book." With the word *book,* he rifled through his backpack and brought out his copy of *Romeo and Juliet.*

"You got to have a secret."

Rene touched his chin and looked skyward dramatically. He then shivered once as his gaze leveled and directed a soft kiss on her lips.

"I like that," purred Marisa, who had accepted the kiss with her eyes open.

"That was one of my secrets. That was the kind of kiss I used to plant on my pillow."

"You kissed your pillow?"

"I slobbered all over it." He laughed with his hand over his mouth.

After his giggling subsided, he opened the copy of *Romeo and Juliet* and said, "Let's practice."

So they sang, out of tune,

"That fair for which love groan'd for and
would die,
With tender Juliet match'd, is now not fair.
Now Romeo is beloved and loves again,
Alike bewitched by the charm of looks..."

They sang the long chorus three times, and before the fourth time Rene brought out his recorder from his backpack.

"With music," Rene suggested. He licked his lips and began to play.

"I'm in love," Marisa told herself. Poetry and music! Her life had changed all because of Alicia and Roberto. If they hadn't got into the car accident, none of this would have happened. This was one of her secrets. Another was that she had liked Roberto a lot, but that was a long, long time ago.

Aunt Sara came over for dinner. She arrived lugging a bag of oranges from the tree in her yard. Marisa gave her aunt a kiss and pried the bag from her.

That night they ate the tamales Marisa's mother had defrosted.

Her mother couldn't help saying, "A young man came by to see Marisa today."

"Mom!" Marisa scolded. She felt her cheeks burn.

"But it's true," her mother remarked.

Marisa's father shook his head at his wife, who grumbled, "Okay, I won't say anything." She parted her tamale and pretended to be hurt.

They ate in silence for only a few minutes before Marisa said, "He's a boy from school. We're in a play."

Her aunt's eyes shone. "That's nice."

"We're going to be in a performance at school. You should come and see it."

"I will." Her aunt reached for the basket filled with tortillas wrapped in a dish towel. "What play, sweetheart?"

Marisa pinched up a glob of *frijoles* in a piece of tortilla and shoved the untidy portion into her mouth. She chewed and chewed and wondered whether she should tell them—they were all waiting for her answer. She swallowed, drank from her water glass, and answered, *"Romeo and Juliet."*

"Oh!" her mother squealed. "How romantic!"

When Marisa's mother said she didn't have to go to work the next day—something about the office building being fumigated—Aunt Sara suggested that her niece stay with her overnight. This way her mother wouldn't have to get up early and drive across town. Marisa could wake up and walk the three blocks to Hamilton Magnet.

"That'll be fun," Marisa said, and ran to her room to get her things. When she snatched her cell phone from the chest of drawers, she saw that she had two messages. She pocketed the cell phone and went to the bathroom for her toothbrush and brush.

Aunt Sara didn't risk asking about Rene, whether he was a friend or if their friendship had advanced to the level of boyfriend and girlfriend. She drove her Volvo station wagon with both hands on the wheel and her eyes flitting up to the rearview mirror every few seconds. She was a cautious driver.

"His name is Rene," Marisa braved.

"That's a nice name. I knew a girl from school named Renée."

They drove in silence for two blocks before her aunt said, "I saw you had a lot of grass on your sweatshirt."

"We were sitting on the grass." Marisa relived the two kisses and had to smile at the image of Rene playing the recorder. "My mom is so embarrassing."

Aunt Sara chuckled. "She is funny."

Marisa reached into her front pocket and brought out her cell phone. She had two more messages.

"But he's your *novio, qué no*?"

Novio. Marisa hadn't applied that Spanish-language distinction. But, yes, she answered her favorite aunt, he was her *novio.*

"And you're really going to be in this play, *verdad*?" Her aunt braked as the light turned yellow.

"Yeah, but we don't have any lines. We just sing in the chorus." She shoved her cell phone back into her pocket.

"'Just sing'? Singing is everything." She gunned the engine when the light turned green. Aunt Sara began to sing a Mexican song, and Marisa was lulled by the song of a young woman who loses her boyfriend to another girl.

That won't happen to me, Marissa thought. *Rene will always be mine.*

At Aunt Sara's house, Marisa showered and then put on her jeans and a T-shirt with the Simpsons on the front. In the steamy bathroom, she checked her messages.

"It's me," the first one said. "Me" was Alicia, asking why Marisa wanted to keep fighting Roberto. The second was from Alicia, too, saying she was sorry for the first phone call.

"Oh, god," Marisa moaned. Couldn't Alicia see that Roberto was no good?

She checked the third message.

"It's me!" It was Rene, who told her about a PBS program on television about volcanoes until his mother's voice—the voice was harsh—told him to get off the phone.

The fourth message was Rene, too. He was singing a made-up tune for "Good night, sleep tight, don't let the bed bugs bite."

Marisa clicked off the phone feeling happy. But she had to wonder about Rene's mother, a dragon by the sound of her voice. Was this his secret? She played back the last message of Rene singing, and then she joined her aunt in the living room for an evening of chess—Marisa was determined to learn a few moves to improve her game.

Chapter

Because they didn't have speaking parts in *Romeo and Juliet*, Marisa and Rene didn't have to show up at many rehearsals. Rene introduced her to chess club and science club meetings, where she clamped her mouth shut and tried to keep from yawning. Bored, she did her homework during the meetings and started a journal that she kept for three days. One day she wrote, "I'm hungry, I mean, really hungry." She mused about food all day. She sensed weakness in her fingers when she wrote that line and later used her famished state as an excuse to give up her journal. She just couldn't write. She was delirious from hunger. How she would have loved to poke a straw into a thick strawberry shake and suck to her heart's content.

She had gone on a diet of fruit and cereal, though when her mother served heavy dishes like lasagna, her nostrils flared and her mouth watered. She would ask her mother to serve her a small portion, and then complain that she meant small but not *that* small. She avoided potato chips and cookies, two temptations that appeared in her dreams. She avoided that tub of chocolate ice cream in the freezer and the crumbly Mexican *queso de cotija.* Instead, she ate apples and oranges, and cracked open pomegranates full of jewels that bled bittersweet juice as she chewed. She bought an overpriced bag of unsalted sunflower seeds, ate a portion of its contents, and threw the rest to the sparrows.

She was losing weight, but her resolve to stay on the diet was tested when Rene suggested trick-or-treating together. She had given up that fall ritual two years ago—too babyish. But she missed dressing up in costumes that she assembled from boxes of clothes in the garage, and missed the sound of candy falling into a grocery bag.

"I'm going to go as a nerd," Rene said, straight-faced, before he erupted in laughter.

"But, Rene, you're a nerd all the time!" Marisa laughed and begged him to please keep his cell phone in his pocket, not on his belt. She hugged him, called him "my precious *nerdito,*" and told him how proud she was that he had retired his white socks.

But neither went trick-or-treating. Rene had to hand out candy at his house, and Aunt Sara asked Marisa to do the same at her place. Aunt Sara was working the night shift at the hospital and didn't want to leave her house empty on a night when not only goblins and spirits but downright nasty thieves broke into homes. She left Marisa with a pizza and three bags of candy to hand out.

"I shouldn't," she told herself as she pulled a cheesy slice of pizza toward her mouth. "I really shouldn't." But her tongue rolled out, and she bit into the slice. Her eyes fluttered closed. It was too delicious. She took a second and third bite and then wiped her fingers on a paper napkin when she heard the shuffling of little feet at the front door. When the doorbell rang, she snatched a bag of candy from the coffee table.

"Trick or treat!" screamed three girls, all princesses.

Marisa rained big chunky candies into their bags, and showered more into the bags of the next herd of trick-or-treaters.

She was kept busy. When the hordes finally stopped coming, she returned to the kitchen with her mouth watering for her half-eaten slice of pizza It had grown cold and gooey, so she popped it in the microwave and returned to the front door when the bell rang.

"Trick or treat," a crew of three guys croaked, their deep voices sounding like frogs.

"Hey," one of them said after he grabbed three fistfuls of candy. "Ain't you Marisa?"

They're from Washington, she guessed.

"Yeah. Who are you?"

The guy stripped off his mask. It was a screaming face, modeled after a painting that had been popular since he was a baby. But he was no longer little, though his pants were riding low. He had a faint mustache and his teeth were yellowish from cigarette smoke.

"Joel," Marisa said. "Aren't you too old for trick-or-treating?"

"*¡Chale!* I could do it two more years." He threw two fingers up like a pitchfork. "After that I'll give it a rest, and then when I get my kids, I'll push them in the stroller."

"*¡Qué gacho, carnal!*" one of the friends cried with laughter.

Joel's friends stripped off their masks. Marisa recognized one of them, and the other was someone she had never met and would rather not know—a chain of bluish tattooed tears fell from the corner of his right eye.

"You moved, *qué no*? Is this your crib?" Joel asked as he leaned around Marisa and peered in. "I like the couch. *Es muy firme* for, *tú sabes,* a little action."

"It's my aunt's place."

"Your *tía* home?"

"Yeah, she's home." Marisa's heart began to thump. Joel wasn't the worst guy in the world, but he wasn't an altar boy, either.

"Too bad," Joel crowed as he wiggled his hips and threw his arms into the air. "We coulda partied. You feel me?" He brought a cigarette out of his shirt pocket and lit up. "Hey, how come you moved to that *gabacho* school? Don't you like us losers?"

Marisa thought fast and conjured up a lie. "My mom made me. She said I was messing up."

"I'm messing up, but my mom don't move me." Joel giggled. "But that's smart of your mom, caring about you and everything." He sucked on his cigarette and let out a wafer of smoke. "The word is you're all stuck-up, too good for us." Joel's face became slick with meanness, his teeth like rows of corn. He turned his face slightly and spit out a flake of tobacco.

"People spew all kinds of nasty rumors," Marisa said with a sneer that had no feeling behind it. She was praying for a group of trick-or-treaters to come up the walk, but none did.

"I heard about you and Roberto. You two threw some *pleitos* and you messed him up good. He's a weak *pendejo,* but you're tight, girl." He turned to his friends. "She's tight, huh?"

The friends nodded like those toy Chihuahuas in the back windows of cars. One took the cigarette from Joel and used it to light his own. The tip of the cigarette caught and glowed red as sin.

Marisa couldn't think of a smooth escape. She looked back into the living room and said, "My aunt wants me."

"You all right, girl," Joel slurred. He turned to his friends. "She's all right, huh?"

Their heads did the toy-Chihuahua nod.

They left tripping down the walk and unwrapping candy bars, their masks sitting on top of their heads. *They don't need masks,* Marisa thought. *They're already scary.*

"You're tight, girl!" All the next day the phrase played in Marisa's mind and made her hate Joel and his low-life friends. *"You're tight, girl!"* echoed again

like a refrain and made her hate the world. *You want to be happy,* she thought, *and then a weasel-neck like Joel shows up to make you feel bad. To make you think nothing has changed at all.*

When Rene and Marisa went to rehearsals for *Romeo and Juliet,* Marisa felt out of place. Everyone was so cheerful, hugging one another and clasping hands. They were *so* touchy-feely.

"They're a bunch of fakes," Marisa muttered. She had just watched the scene when Juliet discovers Romeo dead—Marisa could see the dead Romeo's eyes fluttering. And he had crossed his legs. A dead person crossing his legs? Even their love for each other seemed fake.

"No, they're not. They're as genuine as you or me." Rene pouted with his head down, as if he were mad at his shoes. He asked, "What's wrong with you? How come you're so negative?"

Marisa was hurt. She could take a punch from Roberto, or a slap from a girl with a bad attitude. She could take her mother's scolding voice about her not cleaning up her bedroom. But the questions from Rene hurt. So he thought she had a bad attitude?

"Nothing's wrong with me." Her back stiffened with anger.

"I know that you went to a bad high school—"

Marisa cut Rene off with a bitter stare. She got

up and left the auditorium, her backpack feeling like it carried something heavier than books.

"These Hamilton kids don't know the real world," she muttered as she stood in the autumn sunlight, the wind flicking her hair about her. She took out her cell phone and checked the time: 4:17 P.M. Her mother was going to pick her up at 5:00 in front of the school. Marisa turned, faced the auditorium door where she had exited, and waited for Rene to come out, apologizing on his knees. But the door didn't swing open. She made out laughter coming from inside. Were they laughing at her?

Marisa was sensitive to criticism and she knew that at times she imagined things—a mere glance from someone on the street caused her to roll her hands into fists. *Is it me?* she often thought, and she thought it at that moment: *Is it me? Or is it this new school?* Her mood was dark. She wanted to kick something.

"Maybe I am negative," she muttered. "But I don't care. I don't belong here."

Marisa walked down a hallway plastered with signs for the school clubs—science, vegan, bisexual, poets for the world, thespians, Latinos in business. She sneered at the posters. At her old school the walls were tagged with graffiti.

"I know they're fakes," Marisa said. She boiled

with anger and ventured into the restroom. With a fingernail, she dabbed at something in her eye, which could have been dust, an eyelash, a wind-blown speck from a tree. She blinked, but her eye still felt scratchy. She closed her eyes and reconstructed the image of Rene asking her, "What's wrong with you?" She could have asked him the same, "What's wrong with *you*?" *Sure,* she thought, *he's changed his socks and pants, but not that stupid laugh of his.*

A girl entered the restroom, observed Marisa, and went into a stall, where she started crying. Marisa was going to tease her hair, but she put her brush back. She listened as the crying eventually subsided into a sob, then tiptoed to the stall, knocked, and asked, "You okay? What's wrong?"

There was silence before the girl replied, "Everything."

"What do you mean?" Marisa asked after a long minute.

The girl unlocked the stall and came out. Her eyes were runny with tears and her nose was red.

"This boy I like . . . ," the girl began softly. "He walks past me like he doesn't see me." Tears began to leak down her cheeks.

"Boys!" Marisa growled. "They ain't nowhere like us girls."

Marisa opened her arms and the girl took baby steps into Marisa's embrace. Marisa let her sob on her shoulder and began to think that maybe this touchy-feely approach of her classmates could be real.

"What's your name?" Marisa asked when the crying slowed down.

"Priscilla," the girl sobbed.

"Mine's Marisa," she volunteered, and released the girl from her embrace. She pulled a paper towel from the dispenser and handed it to Priscilla, who blew long and hard and tossed the wadded-up paper towel at the garbage can. She missed by a foot.

They left the restroom, arm in arm, and Marisa couldn't believe the change in herself. Less than an hour before she had been brooding about the actors and their fake expressions of love. Now she could see how she might have been wrong.

"Boys...," Marisa grumbled. "We just got to depend on ourselves."

Whatever had been in her eye was gone. She could see clearly in the late afternoon sun. She realized that it was okay to hug. There was nothing fake about it if it felt right.

Chapter

The next morning Marisa spotted Rene slurping from a water faucet. She was shocked to see that he was back to wearing white socks and high-water pants. His hair was uncombed. His large watch was like a handcuff on his skinny wrist. He was carrying a small briefcase that Marisa knew held his chessboard and pieces. He stood up, wiping droplets from his mouth, and turned away.

Marisa was hurt. How could he so cruelly ignore her?

"So what if he thinks he's better than me?" she muttered as she bumped along a crowded hallway, like a fish swimming against the current. "I don't care about no stupid boy."

But she did care. In history her mind floated

over battle scenes from the American Civil War. In biology she peered into a microscope and attempted to sketch the cells of dead leaves. In English she scrawled on her binder and studied her classmates, some of whom were listening to the teacher discuss a Robert Frost poem about walking through snow. What did she know about snow? She had seen it in calendars, but had never scooped it up and patted it into a ball. She wanted to return to her old school.

But her doubts left her when at lunchtime she saw Priscilla seated alone at a rickety wooden table. When she plopped down opposite Priscilla, she noticed the table was scarred with names of couples: *Terry & Jason, Seth & Brittany, Laura & Rafael, Ryan & Derek.*

"How do you feel?" Marisa asked when her gaze lifted from the table.

Priscilla was eating a large sugar doughnut. She offered half to Marisa.

"Better," Priscilla answered. She nibbled her doughnut and asked Marisa if she was new to the school.

"Yeah, I am. I got tired of all the jargon at my old school." Marisa told her that she had transferred two weeks before because her old school was messed up. She recounted the story of Alicia and Roberto, the accident, the photo that popped out of the glove compartment, and Alicia's broken leg. But she didn't describe the two fights with Roberto—Marisa didn't want to come off as a hothead. She told Priscilla that she moved to the new school to get away from trouble and to get better grades and—she slowly peeled a sliver from the wooden table—because she wanted to be with her new boyfriend.

"Who's he?" Priscilla asked.

Marisa hesitated, swallowing twice as she debated whether to describe Rene, a confirmed nerd. She held the sliver of wood between her thumb and index finger, and slowly applied pressure until a spark of pain ignited against her skin. "It's a guy named Rene."

"Rene Carey?" Priscilla asked.

"No, Rene Torres," Marisa answered without looking at Priscilla. She wanted to give Priscilla time to wince, smirk, or throw up at the mention of Rene the nerd. But she didn't spew to Priscilla that they had just broken up.

Priscilla remained silent. A sparrow landed near their feet in search of crumbs. The bird pecked at something on the ground and flew away.

"He's nice," Priscilla said.

She's so polite, Marisa thought, and laughed. "It's funny how we met." Here Marisa became honest. "You know how I mentioned Alicia and Roberto?"

Current Check-Outs summary for PAFFUMI,
Thu Jul 03 14:08:58 EDT 2014

BARCODE: 20702532634
TITLE: To all the boys I've loved before
DUE DATE: Jul 17 2014

BARCODE: 31251003333046
TITLE: Accidental love / Gary Soto.
DUE DATE: Jul 31 2014

Priscilla nodded.

"Well, I got in a fight with Roberto."

"You mean like—" Priscilla lifted up her two dainty fists.

"Yeah, like that." She told Priscilla how the cell phones had been mixed up in the scuffle.

"Life's weird, huh?" Priscilla remarked. "But how did Roberto know Rene? They go to different schools."

"Rene was tutoring Roberto in math. Roberto has to be better at it to get into the army." Marisa peeled another sliver from the tabletop. "Then we got together to get our cell phones back. I could see that he was a nerd."

"Yeah, he is."

"But he was sort of sweet."

"Sweet matters. That's what I found out when I liked this other boy who turned out to be mean."

"And that's how we started. That's why I'm here." Talking about Rene made Marisa realize that she missed him.

Priscilla and Marissa punched each other's number into their cell phones. The bell rang, and lunch was over for them but just beginning for the sparrows. The birds swooped down from the bare trees to feast on the crumbs students had dropped thoughtlessly to the ground.

"Rene!" Marisa yelled as she pushed through a crowd at the end of the school day. He was hurrying away from her. "I'm going to get real mad if you don't stop. Rene! Rene! Do you hear me?"

Rene stopped, turned, and asked, "What?" One of his pants cuffs was hooked on his sock.

With long scissoring steps, Marisa closed in on him and pulled up within inches of his face.

"How come you're cold to me? Just because I said those people were fake?" She pointed in the direction of the auditorium.

"It's complicated," Rene answered vaguely.

"Complicated!" She breathed in and out like a prizefighter. "Listen, Rene, I was wrong. I was stupid, you know. But it doesn't mean you have to dump me."

"I'm not dumping you." He let his backpack slide from his arm. "It's just that my mom found out about you. And she doesn't want me to see you." His lower lip dropped, as if he couldn't believe what he had just admitted.

"Your mom! What does she have to do with us?" If Marisa were a dragon, smoke would have billowed from her nostrils. "Aren't you a man?"

"No, not yet."

¡Chihuahua! Marisa thought. Of course he wasn't—but still! Then she remembered his mother's unpleasant voice on the telephone. Maybe she was mean as a snake. She risked asking, "You got issues with your mom, huh?"

Head bowed, he answered, "Sometimes."

Marisa's lips rolled and puckered, opened and closed, as anger brewed inside her. When she sighed, some of the anger escaped. She felt sorry for Rene. He had been trying to change, with his clothes and by lifting weights.

"Listen, I have to go," said Rene. He cut a glance at the student parking lot jammed with cars.

"You didn't bring your bike?" Marisa asked. "No, your mom's picking you up. Rene, you're like a little kid!"

Rene squeaked a good-bye, turned, and hurried to the parking lot, where he got into a white Toyota.

"He's not going to just drop me like that!" Marisa ran after the Toyota creeping through the parking lot. Other cars were slowly exiting, turning right because if they went left, a motorcycle cop parked at the corner would twitch his mustache and get them.

"Hey!" She knocked on the window. "Rene, roll down your window."

Rene glanced at her briefly and then stared straight ahead. His hands were fidgeting on his lap. His mother, Marisa guessed, was a control freak.

"Come on—roll it down, Rene." The Toyota slowly advanced toward the exit—the parking lot was crowded with cars trying to get out at the same time—and Marisa kept pace as she considered the dramatic action of leaping onto the hood. But she didn't have to. The window slid down noiselessly.

"My mom says what do you want?" Rene asked meekly.

"What! Rene, you're talking to me—your girlfriend!" Marisa cut her attention to Rene's mother, who was a little older than her own mom. Her hair was stiff with hair spray, and her small mouth held back large white teeth. The dress was too short for a woman her age—the hemline revealed two knobby knees.

"Your *what*?" Rene's mother barked. She braked the car, an action that made Rene's head sway forward and his arms rise up against the dash.

"*Mi novio!* You know, like we hold hands," Marissa blurted out. Her temper flared. What was the big deal for Rene to have a girlfriend?

"He is no way your *novio*! He's my son!" She bared a set of shark's teeth.

"Wow, girl," Marisa sang. "Don't get so blown up. We're not getting married or anything."

"I'm not a *girl,* as you say!" She snarled something in Spanish that Marisa couldn't make out. Nor could Marisa make out a phrase shaped on Rene's lips—*I love you? I like you?* Or was it *I leave you*?

It must have been the last phrase, because when the Toyota pulled away with a screech, Rene, apparently loyal to his mother, didn't turn back like a little boy for even one last look.

Marisa rode the city bus home that day. At red lights she peered out the window, greasy with fingerprints, and observed the drivers, men and women, some adolescents a year or two older than she, all going somewhere, all with their own cargo of problems, and maybe joys that brought light to their eyes. Marisa wished she could write a song to explain her feelings—a nerdy boyfriend gone, a new school, a new friend named Priscilla with her own issues.

"Is there anything wrong?" an elderly woman asked. Her eyes seemed moist.

"No, not really," Marisa answered. She could sense the woman had been watching her, a kind woman with her coat buttoned all the way up. Her grayish hair was tidy, and the cat pin on her lapel sparkled every time the bus hit a pothole. She was squeezing a sheer silk handkerchief. Marisa recognized that the woman was trying to be nice.

Marisa got off the bus two stops early and kicked through the leaves. When she arrived home, tired and heavy at heart, she discovered Alicia waiting on the porch. Her crutches were leaning on the rail. Two cold sodas, both unopened, stood sweaty at her feet.

"Alicia!" Marisa called happily. She was glad to see her, this old friend who was like a new friend. They had known each other since second grade, and wasn't it true that they had traded sandwiches? Wasn't that the sign of true friendship, the sharing of food and the ritual stomping of empty milk cartons?

"I heard what happened at the car wash," Alicia said, and pouted. She rose stiffly, one hand on the porch rail.

"Stop bothering me. It's over," Marisa said. "How did you get here?"

"Mom brought me. I told her you and me had some studying to do." Alicia said that she and her mother had had a long talk about boys. Her mother told her she trusted her to use her head and said that the episode with Roberto was a learning experience.

Marisa didn't relish talking about Roberto. She said, "Let me have one of those sodas."

"Cream or root beer?" Alicia asked.

"*La crema,* girl."

They drank their sodas on the lawn. Alicia's blue cast attracted two boys riding their bikes down the street. They stopped and asked about the cast. Alicia, straight-faced, said she'd got into a skiing accident. The boys looked at each other.

"What's snow like?" the taller of the two asked. Marisa and Alicia could see that he must have been eating a lot of candy, because his tongue was coated. He had sucked something sweet and blue, and the corners of his mouth were still stained. He was a kid living through the sense of taste.

"Like real cold fire," Marisa answered for Alicia.

Alicia nodded. "That's right. That's why if you stay in snow too long, it makes your skin all red."

The boys rode away. Marisa knew that the boys—*chavalos,* as her father would call them—were built for play and didn't want to stand around discussing fiery snow. They were gone, weaving down the pitted road, where dogs lurked beyond rickety fences.

The girls laughed and clinked their soda cans

together. Neither had ever seen snow, but they imagined that it was like a cold fire. They had imagined a lot of things when they were really young, but never a fight that could end their friendship.

Alicia swept her leg toward Marisa.

"You be the first."

"First what?"

Marisa understood when Alicia handed her a Sharpie pen. She wrote on the cast: "Alicia & Marisa—*siempre*."

They were friends, they were girlfriends, they were *hermanas* with different last names. They sat on the grass talking about family and boys until dusk crept up the street and Marisa's father's truck pulled into the driveway, fenders rattling and horn tooting.

"My dad will give you a ride home in a little bit," Marisa said, and pulled Alicia to her feet. "Come in for a while."

"Go get my crutches," Alicia begged like a little girl.

"Forget your crutches!" Marisa picked her up in her arms, and Alicia said, "Dang, you're strong."

"You're light," Marisa said. "Hey, did you see that I lost weight?"

"Oh, yeah? How did you do it?"

"I stopped with the *chicharrones*," she huffed as she carried Alicia to the porch, where her father was unlacing his cement-dusted work boots. "I think I just kept my mouth shut and nothing went in—that's my diet!"

Chapter

Rene avoided Marisa as he maneuvered down the hallways, his attention drawn toward the ground and the vista of legs, shoes, stains of spilled soda, hardened gum, and pennies that weren't worth the effort of students too cool to pick them up. Marisa recognized his sadness and was waiting for the Thursday rehearsal of *Romeo and Juliet* to apologize. She hoped that the showdown in the school parking lot hadn't got him in even more trouble. At rehearsal they would have to stand side by side and could spy on each other out of the corners of their eyes. She would try to clutch his hand and not give it back.

On Wednesday, Hamilton Magnet was scheduled to play Washington in basketball, a preseason tune-up between two teams that both played as if their shoelaces were undone—sloppy. The players for Hamilton were mostly anemic-looking poets and artists, a few math-heads strong at calculating their chances of victory (zero), and some musicians from the orchestra. The tuba player, Marcos Sanchez, was the shortest player on the team—five foot three, red-cheeked after three minutes on the court, and slow as syrup drooling from a bottle of Mrs. Butterworth. He ran up and down the court as if he were carrying his tuba and a folding chair.

"Come with me," Priscilla begged as she captured one of Marisa's wrists and shook her arm like a garden hose. Marisa agreed.

At the game, held in Hamilton's gymnasium, the two girls arrived just as a crew of students from Washington came in, all loud, all jabbing their hands into potato chip bags.

"Hey, girl!" Latisha loudly greeted Marisa when they met at the folding table where tickets were sold. She had a comb stuck in her Afro. "What you doin' here?"

Marisa and Latisha had been close friends in first and second grades, but by third grade they had drifted—Latisha to her black friends at one table in the lunchroom and Marisa to the Latinos hanging out on a grassy hill. It was a division of races. It was the way things were no matter how much the teachers tossed around the word *multicultural.*

"Hey, Latisha." Marisa hugged her old friend. "This is my new school."

"New school!" Latisha was not known to speak softly. She didn't do anything softly. "What you mean? You ain't gonna sit with us?" Her face rolled with dissatisfaction. "If that's the case, we gonna spank your team's booty. We be pumped!"

Marisa waved and smiled, and looped her arm into Priscilla's as they paid their two dollars, entered the gymnasium, and climbed the bleachers.

The coach, with a gut as round as a basketball, stood on the sidelines—he was Mr. Greene, Marisa's math teacher, who looked like he couldn't move but was surprisingly swift on his feet. The vice principal was on his cell phone. Three or four teachers, plus a security guard in a yellow jacket, were trying to pin a school banner to a wall. A few students were clotted together and a few sat in the top row of the bleachers.

"I've never been to a basketball game," Marisa told Priscilla, who said, "No, sir, you been to a game before," and then screamed when the DJ started a song that she really liked.

"It's true. I've been to football games, but never

a basketball game." Marisa scanned the gym. "It's kinda sorry, huh? There ain't hardly anybody here."

The school's flag, high in the rafters, was stirred by the air-conditioning. One of the lights flickered, and somewhere outside a door was banging shut again and again.

"So which one is he?" Marisa asked, taking a chocolate-flavored Tootsie Roll Pop that Priscilla offered her.

"That hottie there," Priscilla said. She pointed quickly, and had to point again when Marisa, with candy on her tongue, slurred, "Which one?"

"The one with the ball. Aaron."

Marisa studied Priscilla's would-be boyfriend as she sucked on the candy. He was average height, dark haired, and pale as milk. His biceps bulged with muscles. He had a star-shaped tattoo on the back of his right calf.

"He's hella cute," Marisa remarked.

"I know," Priscilla responded after a long span of silence. She chewed at a fingernail and then scowled at it. "I'm such a mess. Even my fingers are bleeding."

"Stop it then!" Marisa slapped Priscilla's hand, and Priscilla let it drop onto her thigh.

Marisa's own heart leaped when she noticed

Rene at a long table. At first she thought he was working the soundboard, but saw that he kept glancing up at the scoreboard over by the far end of the double doors.

"Rene's here, too," Marisa remarked flatly.

"Where?" Priscilla asked.

"There." She pointed, slightly embarrassed because Rene was wearing a pair of high-water pants, and from where she sat she could tell his socks didn't match. She sighed and said, "Man, his clothes are so wickity-wack."

When the game started, the small group of Washington supporters began to rock as if they were riding a bus, then shriek when one of the players scored, and were louder than Hamilton's pep band. They blew up their potato chip bags and clapped them when a Hamilton player was set to shoot.

It was 10–0 before Hamilton scored, helped out by a Washington player who accidentally tipped the ball into the opponent's basket.

Marisa watched Aaron play. He moved nicely on the court, and he seemed to care whether they won or lost. He hustled, and one of every three of his shots swished. When he was taken out of the game, he scrubbed his face with a towel and drank three cups of water. Marisa was fascinated by him—

she had to admit that he was good-looking, even gorgeous, and then she felt hideous about such a thought. Was she coveting the boy Priscilla liked?

"So what does he do?" Marisa asked. In her three weeks at Hamilton, she had discovered that everyone did something—computer graphics, robotics, poetry, drama, homemade graphic novels, and lots of music, both classical and alternative.

"He plays basketball," she answered. "He lives and dies for it."

"You got it bad, huh, girl?"

"Yeah, real bad. When I'm in bed I send him these telepathic messages. I tell him to look for me—Priscilla."

They both laughed, but Priscilla laughed harder.

"He knows, but he doesn't care," Priscilla added. She told Marisa that his parents were both doctors. That much she knew about his family life.

Marisa paid attention to some of the game, but mostly she spent time looking at the back of Rene's head as he worked the electronic scoreboard. She felt childish as she rummaged through her memories of their first—and only?—fight. All she had spewed from her lips was that she thought the actors were fake. And all he had said was, "How come you're so negative?" Her ego was fragile as a robin's egg, and it broke. She wished she could take back her bitterness. She liked him. After all, hadn't he been willing to punch Roberto for her?

Marcos Sanchez only played two minutes of the first half, and during halftime he joined the pep band, his face growing sweatier from his tuba playing than from the time on the court. He did his best to keep in tune to the rally cry of "Louie, Louie."

Hamilton lost 65–23.

On Thursday morning clouds rolled in and darkened the autumn sky. Rain splashed like tears against the kitchen window, trying to get in and spread its moodiness. Marisa was considering what to wear—a jacket or just two sweatshirts—as she raked a thin layer of strawberry jam over an unbuttered piece of toast. Her cell phone rang. It was Priscilla, whose first words were, "I had a dream that he was talking to me." She didn't have to explain the cryptic message.

"He's on you. He's trailing you like a shark."

"I hope he bites," she said, and hung up.

When Marisa got to school, Rene seemed to be waiting for her. He was kicking the scuffed toe of his shoe into the asphalt.

"Hey," Marisa greeted. She could have played hard to get and hooked herself to the crowd heading toward the cafeteria, but she emptied her heart. She was full of words that needed to come out.

"Hey," Rene greeted. "I want to say I'm sorry."

"No, I'm sorry."

They stood just inches away from each other. Marisa could smell soap on Rene. She could also smell coffee, a surprise because he was vegan—and didn't they oppose caffeine?

"I should have been braver," Rene muttered.

Marisa paused as she nearly blurted out, "Why is your mom like a hag?" The urge was so great that she had already inhaled a lungful of wind for such a purpose. Instead, she let it out by muttering, "I didn't know you drink coffee."

"Just sometimes," Rene said before he began to explain what was in his heart. "Listen, Marisa, my mom is real strict. She wants me to, you know, do well in school." He flapped his arms at his sides as if he were a penguin. "She wants me to go to Harvard or Stanford."

Here it comes, Marisa thought. *He's going to cut me loose.*

"She thinks having a girlfriend will get me in trouble."

"Do you think I'm trouble?" Marisa asked. She rested her head against his shoulder, eyes closed, and smelled his soap. Or was it shaving cream? Had he started to shave?

"Yeah, I do," he answered.

Marisa pulled her head away from his shoulder.

"So I'm trouble?" Her system began to cook up a pot of anger.

"Marisa! Let me finish!" He fumed for a moment, and finally said in a controlled voice, "I like you because you are trouble. It's dangerous. Don't forget that was the first time I got into a fight—ever!"

Marisa had first raised her fists when she was in her stroller and her older cousin José had ripped a Popsicle from her sticky fingers. Or at least that is what she was told every time she saw her cousin, now an army sergeant and the push-up king of his battalion. This cousin—and Marisa had witnessed it—could do three hundred two-finger push-ups and hardly break a sweat.

"I know it's sad, but that's me." Rene twitched his nose. "It doesn't hurt anymore."

Marisa brought herself close again. The soap smell was there, and the coffee smell, plus something—she sniffed like a rabbit—like sadness. *Poor baby,* she mused. *He wants to be a man.*

"Rene," Marisa asked.

"What?"

"You're standing on my shoe." She played it up by wincing from pain. She took a few stumbling steps as she pretended to make it better.

He lifted his shoe and said, "Oh, I'm *so* sorry."

"Listen, buddy boy," Marisa said as she stroked his hair. "You're not supposed to say that you're sorry all the time."

"I'm not?" Rene appeared baffled.

"No, you're not. You're the dude, the guy, *el mero mero, ese vato,* the homey, the heavyweight champion of this girl's heart." Marisa touched her heart. "You're El Macho, Mr. Suave, and if you keep lifting weights, contender for the title of Mr. America."

Rene sucked in his gut so that his chest stood out.

"Remember, you wear *los pantalones,*" Marisa said, then grimaced at his high-waters. "But I'm gonna tell you what kind. And it ain't the ones you got on!"

The two kissed and made up and lifted weights that day in the abandoned part of the gym. Marisa did a hundred sit-ups, and for the fun of it lifted Rene into her arms and staggered about. "This is just to let...," she huffed, "this is just to let you know that if you..." She adjusted him in her arms and groaned, "If you ever get sick or in an accident, I'll carry you to the hospital."

After school they went to rehearsal. They didn't have much to do. The chorus stood on the side of the stage, and the director, with his hands in his hair, scolded, "Romeo, your timing is all wrong."

Marisa elbowed Rene and winked at him.

"Who wears the pants?" she murmured.

"I do," he answered.

"And you have to speak clearly," the director boomed. "Remember not to swallow your words. Take your time."

"But who tells you what kind, my Romeo?" Marisa whispered in his ear.

"You do." He laced his fingers into hers and smiled.

After rehearsal they met with Priscilla and the three of them went to a mall close to Marisa's aunt's house. There the girls pulled Rene into a store filled with loud bass-thumping music. None of the words were decipherable.

"But I'm the man," he protested over the music. "The man!"

The girls giggled.

"You wish!" Marisa laughed. "Right now Priscilla and me are the mommies, and we're going to buy bad baby a pair of pants."

They had pooled their money and borrowed some from one of Priscilla's friends. They came up with twenty-nine dollars, just enough to splurge on a pair of jeans in the current style.

When they found the right jeans, Rene headed for the dressing rooms. He emerged lamenting, "But they don't fit!" He gripped the loose front and remarked that he looked like the after photo of a formerly fat person. "Anyhow, they look like someone else wore them for a million years. They're faded."

"That's how you're supposed to wear them," Priscilla retorted.

"They're too long," he added as he modeled in front of a mirror. "They're going to drag."

"What did I say to you?" Marisa asked.

"I wear the pants."

"¿Y qué más?"

"But you pick them out?"

"Dang, he's trained." Priscilla laughed.

The girls bought the jeans for him. One on each side, they escorted him like police from the store, Rene giggling and protesting that he hardly knew these two females and would someone please, please help him, because his pants were falling off.

Chapter

Marisa stopped just short of stalking Aaron into the boys' restroom during lunch on Friday. She would have but for the two boys lurking like vultures at the entrance, their hands stuffed in their front pockets. She waited by the drinking fountain and pressed her hand over her heart. Its engine was steady. She found herself feeling better about her plan.

When Aaron came out, hitching up his pants, she said, "Hey, pretty boy, come here."

Aaron looked at her as if she were a bug and slowly raised a hand to point at his chest.

"That's right—you and your mighty muscles. Bring them over here." She guiltily noted that his chest was so much more endowed than poor Rene's. The boy had game.

"Do I know you?" Aaron asked as he sauntered over, running his hands through his hair.

Marisa ignored his question. "You know, when you shoot, you got to keep your elbows in. And bend those cute knees of yours." She raised her arms into a shooting position and bent her knees. She felt a little stupid, as she knew almost nothing about basketball. She remembered one more piece of advice from her father. "Plus, you can't hold your breath. Got to be natural."

Aaron blinked at her and turned away, hitching up his pants again.

Why does Priscilla like him? Marisa wondered. *And why did Alicia like Roberto? Why do girls fall for such fools?*

She sidled up to Aaron. "Remember, you can't hold your breath. You did that a couple of times at the game on Wednesday," Marisa informed him. As they turned the corner toward the science rooms, she added, in a whisper, "I know a girl who likes you."

That stopped Aaron. Advice on shooting didn't earn his attention, but the mention of a mysterious girl halted his swaggering walk. He turned, licked his thin, pretty lips, and sized up Marisa. His eyes narrowed, and a smile began to form on his face.

He stepped close to her and breathed in her ear, "A lot of girls like me." His bright ironic smile glowed like a lantern. "And thanks for the advice. I'll remember it on the court."

Conceited! Marisa couldn't believe such a boy. Sure, he was drop-dead gorgeous, strong, and maybe had plenty of smart noodles coiled up in his brain. His parents were doctors, right? But he was stuffed like a sausage with himself.

In English Marisa clacked her pencil between her upper and lower teeth, and then bared her teeth to a small compact, her breath fogging the mirror's surface.

"What are you smiling about?" Mr. Warren asked. "You're supposed to be doing your assignment."

"Who, me?" Marisa asked, her compact clicking closed.

"Yes, you, Miss Rodriguez."

"I wasn't smiling. I was just checking to see if I had stuff between my teeth."

A couple of classmates laughed, and Marisa had to smile but with her mouth closed—maybe there *was* gunk stuck between her teeth.

When Marisa was leaving at the end of class, Mr. Warren called her back. "You're distracted," he said. "You need to focus."

"I know," Marisa agreed. "It's just that I'm in love, and I'm also working out my plan to help my friend who's in love."

Mr. Warren didn't want to hear any more.

"Let's not talk about girls and boys and what you're up to." He thumped his pencil against the pile of essays as if he were trying to punish them.

"You must have been in love when you were our age." Marisa had never spoken so boldly to a teacher. At Washington she had been a moody shadow ghosting down the hallway, and she would have never raised her hand in class, even if she had to go to the bathroom. That would have been uncool. But at Hamilton she had begun to see that she could bare her soul.

"Yeah, I was in love," Mr. Warren said, patting the globe of his belly. "With beef enchiladas." He warned her about primping in class and asked how rehearsals were going for *Romeo and Juliet.*

"Like, real neat," she chimed, then paused, hand over her mouth as if it had issued a foul word. She would have to watch that. *Shoot, I might turn into a nerd like Rene,* she thought.

"You talked to him?" Priscilla said into her cell phone outside the library.

"Yeah," Marisa answered. She had just got out

of her last class, biology, where she had splayed open an unfortunate frog (already dead) with a dull knife. She and Rene were going to rendezvous at the auditorium for rehearsal. "Yeah, we were chopping it up. I corrected his outside shot." She had the tickling urge to describe him as she saw him—conceited—but she was certain that would destroy Priscilla or, even worse, make Priscilla defend the blockhead basketball player.

"Oh, god, I can't believe it!" Priscilla screamed. "You talked basketball with him? Oh, wow!"

As Marisa approached the library, she could see Priscilla stomping her feet in excitement and bellowing into her cell phone. "You talked to him? Really? Oh, wow!"

"She's really got it bad," Marisa told herself. "She's really in love." She closed her cell phone as Priscilla was asking if he knew who she was.

"Aaron! Aaron! Aaron!" Marisa teased loudly.

Priscilla's face twisted in terror. Shocked, she ran over from the library and pulled on Marisa's arm. She hauled her away as if she were a bad child. "I can't believe you said his name so loudly. What if he heard?"

"It would be good if he heard. In fact—" Marisa caught sight of a shuffling Aaron, pants hanging low, out of the corner of her eye. "Here he is." She shrugged out of Priscilla's grip and hollered, "Hey, Aaron, remember to keep breathing when you shoot!"

Aaron was with two boys, both players, and he cut loose from them and approached the girls, hitching up his pants. He first sized up Marisa and then Priscilla before asking Marisa, "What's your name?"

"Marisa," Marisa answered. "My boyfriend is Rene. And this is Priscilla. She doesn't have a boyfriend."

Priscilla turned away and nearly doubled over, embarrassed.

"Don't play shy," Marisa advised Priscilla. She wanted to impress upon Aaron that he was dealing with two girls who were not afraid to take chances.

Aaron's smile was more like a snicker.

"Isn't she embarrassing?" Priscilla's face was red, but Marisa thought her blushing gave her a healthy look.

Aaron shrugged.

"We checked you out Wednesday," Priscilla remarked.

Aaron chewed his gum and then asked, "Doing what?"

Priscilla's head tilted downward and then

swung up. "Playing basketball—you were so good!"

Aaron's gum chewing slowed to a stop. "You think I played good?"

Marisa had to have her say. "You are so full of yourself, mister."

Aaron shifted his attention to Marisa, who had clapped her hand over her mouth.

"Marisa!" Priscilla screamed.

Aaron smiled. "She's right. I take after my dad."

"Is your dad full of *pedos,* too?" Marisa nearly asked.

"My dad played in high school." Turning to Priscilla, he asked, "What's your name again?"

¡Ay, Chihuahua! Marisa was disgusted that Mr. Basketball had already forgotten her name.

"Priscilla," she answered. "My dad used to play basketball, too."

Aaron's eyes widened.

"He used to play with my little brother Adam." Priscilla giggled.

Aaron nodded. "Cool."

"I play tennis," Priscilla continued. "I used to be really awful, but I got better. Now I'm just awful."

"You go, girl!" Marisa chirped. "Hey, did you hear the joke about the two cats that went to go see a tennis match?"

Neither had, and neither showed the vaguest interest in hearing it. Marisa staggered back a few steps to give them room as they kept talking.

"Well," Aaron finally said, "I gotta bounce. I'll give you a call."

"But you don't know her number." Marisa stepped between them like a referee.

He got Priscilla's number, then turned and swaggered away to join a clot of boys huddled around a trash can—they were peeling oranges and flicking the peels into it.

"Girl, I could murder you," Priscilla whined under her breath.

"But I got you two talking," Marisa insisted. "And he has your number. You did good. He's going to like you." She hooked her arm into Priscilla's and the two walked toward the auditorium, where she caught sight of Rene and a friend thumb wrestling.

"Can you believe we girls like boys? They're so dumb!" Marisa had to ponder her own instincts. She had met Rene via Roberto, whom she had met through her friend Alicia. But just how had she started liking Rene? It was a mystery—something like chemistry.

Priscilla was nearly skipping at Marisa's side. "I can't believe he talked to me. I'm *so* lucky. How long before you think he'll call?"

Marisa speculated the call would come in three

days. To call any sooner would show that he was hurting for attention. Aaron was too cool to want to give the impression that he was thirsty for excitement, though Marisa was certain that he was salivating over Priscilla. She was cute.

While doing her math in bed on Monday night, an activity that produced one wet yawn after another, Marisa got a call from Rene.

"My mom took my new pants away," he said promptly.

Marisa flung her brick-heavy math book across the bed.

"She what?"

"She says I look like a gangster."

Marisa resisted her typical angry response, which would start with one-word insults and then move to include long fiery sentences. Still, she had to ponder, what kind of mother was she? No wonder Rene was such a nerd.

"Listen, buddy boy, remember you wear *los pantalones.* You're the dude."

"Yeah, I remember," he moaned weakly. "I wear the pants, but you pick out the style and color."

Marisa chuckled. She was teaching her lover boy good.

"You told your mother that Priscilla and me bought them for you, huh?" Marisa asked.

"Yeah, it kinda came out."

Rene was her darling, nerdy boyfriend. She had challenged and beat him at thumb wrestling, and then let him win when she saw how his sweet face got screwed up with pain. She felt sorry for him again.

"Hey...," Marisa started.

"Hay is for horses," Rene quipped. He began his honking laughter.

"Rene, you gotta learn a new way of laughing." She told him he sounded like a goose.

"But I've always laughed like this." He offered another barrage of *honk-honk* laughter followed by a piggy snort.

"It's not time for your silliness," Marisa retorted as she stood up and began pacing her bedroom. "You tell your mom that she did bad."

Silence.

"Are you there?"

"Yeah, I'm here," he said. "My mom is so mean."

"You wear the pants—*recuerdas*? You're the man, *el mero mero*."

Marisa could hear a lumpy swallow in his voice as he confirmed his role: "That's right, I'm the man."

Marisa then asked if he had done his fifty push-ups. A few days before, she had devised an exercise regimen for both of them. Since meeting Rene she had lost inches off her waist and hips, which had drawn suspicion from her mother, who with a mouth full of mashed potatoes had asked, "Are you bulimic?" Marisa had answered no and described her regimen to get skinny—or at least slim down enough so that she could one day put on a dress, something she rarely did.

"No, but I did do six push-ups," Rene admitted.

"Only six?"

"Yeah, that's when Mom came into the room and took my pants off the bed and hid them." There was sorrow in his voice, and even more sorrow when he said he wished that he were like Aaron. Priscilla had crowed and crowed about Aaron, the man about campus. Marisa remembered how Rene's shoulders had sagged, and during rehearsal he had declared that he was no good at any sport, even the nerd's sport—thumb wrestling.

Chapter

On Friday night Marisa stayed over at her aunt's house and talked for hours on the phone: first with Alicia; then with her mother, who called to ask if she wanted to go play bingo at the church (she didn't); then with Roberto, who begged forgiveness for poking Rene in the nose (he didn't apologize for hitting *her*); and last with Priscilla, who squealed that Aaron had asked them to shoot baskets with him on Saturday morning.

Marisa had agreed.

The next morning Rene was on the bar of his bicycle, honking with laughter each time the bike dipped into a pothole.

"Careful, I'm precious cargo," he joked.

"Precious for what?" She was playing with him.

She laughed when he started a coughing fit after a gnat flew down his throat. "Consider that poor little bug your protein."

When the park came into view, Rene panicked. "I'm no good at sports."

Marisa huffed up a hill slick with dew. She caught her breath and said, "What do you mean you're no good at sports? I saw you beat Trung yesterday at thumb wrestling."

"That's because money was involved."

"How much?"

"A quarter per game." He honked with laughter and bragged that he won a dollar off Trung and was prepared to splurge it on a Big Gulp if Marisa could pay the tax.

"Man, you know how to treat a *chola* really nice." She planted a kiss on the back of his neck and asked why he smelled so good.

"I put on some of my mom's perfume." He honked again with laughter. "I don't know why I did that."

"You girl!" When she slapped his arm, she nearly lost control and steered the bike into a set of buckled garbage cans. She secretly thought she wouldn't have minded a crash because it would have brought him to the ground where she could kiss him until he was out of breath.

The park was nearly deserted—an elderly woman was feeding pigeons and far away a man was playing fetch with his dog. A rusty swing squeaked in the autumn breeze.

Rene jumped off the bike and made a sour face at the sight of his socks. One was blue and the other black.

"You're a disaster, buddy boy," Marisa said, clicking her tongue. She tossed the bike aside and gave Rene a hug and a kiss on his lips.

"Guess what?" Rene asked.

"I don't know."

"I forgot to brush my teeth," he answered, and started his honking.

"You *cochino*!" She wiped her mouth on the sleeve of her sweater.

"Nah, just kidding. I brushed them twice. I have ascertained your hunger for my body and figured that you would want to devour it."

"Hunger for your body! You sound like Aaron."

Marisa flung a handful of leaves at him, wrestled him easily to the ground, and planted kisses on his neck and then a long one on his mouth.

"But do you think I'll change? You know, be strong like other guys?" Rene asked after he caught his breath. Before she could answer, he added, "You're so beautiful."

Marisa's heart leaped like a gazelle. "If you change, just make it your socks."

They shook themselves clean of leaves and grass and sat on a bench, holding hands. Marisa confessed that she did possess a desire to change. She had lost weight, that much was true. But she also wanted to be kinder, less likely to explode with anger.

"Less animosity toward mankind, you mean," Rene said.

"Less *what*?"

Rene offered a definition of the word *animosity,* which he said resulted when she called people and moments "stupid."

Marisa studied Rene and smirked. "You think you're all smart."

"But I am!" Rene honked. "I took a pre-SAT exam and I scored great."

Aaron showed up, a basketball under his arm. He was wearing an oversized Los Angeles Lakers jersey. The back read KOBE.

"Hey," Aaron greeted them. His sweats had been dragging in the dirt and the cuffs had picked up a lot of mud.

"Hay is for—"

Marisa punched Rene in the arm. "Don't you dare say it."

"Priscilla's not here?" Aaron asked with his eyes cast on the netless rim.

"She'll be here," Marisa said, and against her better judgment attempted to flatter Aaron by describing a shot he had made against Washington.

"Yeah," he uttered, and did a slow layup.

"Oh, here she comes," chimed Rene.

Priscilla was running up the hill with a beagle on a leash.

"I am *so* late," Priscilla said. She was out of breath, and her face was pink.

Marisa understood why. Priscilla had spent her time dressing. Her hair was done in a ponytail and she was wearing a tight dress. Her lips were shiny with lip gloss.

Aaron gawked at Priscilla and did the best thing that a jock could do to demonstrate he liked someone: He passed her the basketball.

"Thanks," Priscilla said, beaming. She palmed it awkwardly, and laughed when it hit her knee and rolled away. Her beagle chased after it.

"What's your dog's name?" Marisa asked.

"Peaches," Priscilla answered as she retrieved the ball.

"Come on, let's play," Aaron said. "How about you three against me?"

What a jerk, Marisa thought. She prayed that

Priscilla would see him for what he was: a conceited jughead.

"Sounds good to me," Rene said.

Aaron bounced the ball between his legs and faked left, which all three of his opponents bought. He moved swiftly right and finger-rolled the basketball through the rim.

"Oh, wow," Priscilla said. "That was really good."

Aaron bounced the ball and tossed it to Rene, who started toward the basketball. He shot but missed the backboard.

"Hold on, dude," Aaron said. "You got to check the ball. You can't just start shooting. And anyhow, it's my outs. I made the basket."

Marisa's heart was pumping with something that felt like hatred. *Cálmate,* she warned herself. *Chill.*

Rene instinctively handed Aaron the ball, and kept doing it while Aaron scored easily against the three of them. They lost 21–0.

"You're so much better than us," Priscilla said. "Like, we never got to shoot even once."

"Yeah, you did. But you missed." Aaron suggested that he play with only his left hand.

"That sounds fair," Priscilla said giddily. A storm passed over Marisa's eyes—she just didn't like this guy, no matter how handsome he was.

They again lost 21–0, so Aaron suggested that they just watch him do reverse layups.

Marisa fumed. Still, she watched him do one reverse layup after another. He then had Rene feed him balls as he tried to dunk the ball.

"Throw it higher, man," he scolded.

Rene tossed the ball, but each time Aaron complained about the toss until he finally snarled, "Never mind." He glowered at Rene.

"Hey, buster!" Marisa called out. "You think you're so good, why are you on a losing team?"

"'Cause we don't have a center," Aaron snapped back. "I'm gonna go."

Priscilla bowed her head, bit a knuckle, and finally cried, "Can't we just have fun?"

Aaron ignored the painful moment and spun the basketball on the tip of his finger. He did a layup and then said, "I gotta meet some guys." His eyes locked onto Priscilla for a long second as if he wanted to say something meaningful. Instead, he spread his attention to all four of them—the beagle had come to sit at Priscilla's feet—and announced that there was a preseason game coming up. He had free tickets if they wanted.

"*Ay,* how generous," Marisa said sarcastically. "Those tickets—what are they, two whole dollars?—would break us. I don't think I can afford to buy one." She was hot. How she wished Aaron would do a layup into a brick wall. She had forgotten that phrase Rene had taught her earlier—something about antifreeze? No, *animosity*. That was it. She still wasn't sure she knew what the word meant, but she knew she possessed it within her soul. She was mean as a snake and would have spat her venom if Aaron suddenly hadn't wheeled and started jogging away.

The three of them watched his departure until he disappeared from sight.

Monday. Because Marisa was late to biology class, ancient Mr. Carver had her stay after to help him retrieve a cart of books from storage. The students were done with the frogs, done squinting at leaves under a microscope, and done kissing petri dishes and appraising the horrid bacteria spawned a day later. Now he wanted to lecture on fossils.

"And not fossils like me." Mr. Carver chuckled. He was an old man with rivulets of lines around his eyes and mouth. He walked with a stooped shuffle as if he were ready to spin a bowling ball down a polished alley.

Marisa and Mr. Carver ventured into storage While he stepped among the shelves of books,

Marisa noticed a chalkboard on wheels. There was a poorly drawn heart at its center and within the heart a name: *Samantha.* Taped to the edges of the chalkboard were wilted flowers and balloons deflated with age. Someone had written, *We'll miss you.*

"Who's Samantha?" Marisa asked. She had a deep feeling that this girl Samantha was dead and her memory no more than a crooked heart. A shiver rose from her lower back and blossomed in her shoulders.

"Who?" Mr. Carver asked from behind a wall of books.

"Never mind."

Marisa shivered when she touched the chalkboard. She examined the chalk on her finger, chalk as white as bone. She remembered playing dead with her cousin Pilar when they were little, and thinking that it wasn't really all that bad. She couldn't move, but she still had her thoughts.

"What?" Mr. Carver called. He reappeared from behind the wall with a stack of books in his hands.

"Who's Samantha?"

He set the books on the cart and approached the chalkboard, spanking dust from his hands. "I don't recall," he answered.

"I think she died," Marisa said.

Mr. Carver nodded. He peeled one of the cards from the chalkboard and remarked, "Maybe she died of a broken heart. I don't remember her."

Marisa thought of Priscilla. After Aaron left the park, Priscilla had collapsed against Marisa's shoulder to cry. Marisa had patted her on the back and let her new friend sob. "He's no good," Marisa said, and Priscilla had agreed through clenched teeth, "I know, I know." For a second she imagined Priscilla collapsing to the ground, brokenhearted, all because of a conceited boy.

Marisa helped Mr. Carver stack books on the cart. She looked back and wondered how long Samantha's name would remain on the chalkboard before someone—a janitor, a student, or a teacher as ancient as Mr. Carver—would erase her name for good.

Chapter

Marisa stepped out of the shower, felt a bump on her hip, and asked herself, "What the heck is this?" For one frightening moment she thought that it might be a cancerous tumor. She dressed and ran to her mother, who was at the kitchen table about to bite into a jelly doughnut. After her mother felt around Marisa's body, she offered an unprofessional conclusion: It was a hip bone.

"See, you have a shape," her mother praised. Then she raised the doughnut to her mouth, nibbling it delicately with a napkin under her chin in anticipation of the oozing jelly. She swallowed and cleared her throat. "You're turning into a lady. How about we get you a new dress?"

Marisa wasn't quite ready for *that* much change

yet. She declined the dress but did ask for three dollars—it was her turn to treat Rene to one of those fruity drinks at the school snack shop.

For years Marisa had been chubby—*una gordita*—but now she could see that beneath that wobbly fat breathed a shapely young woman. That thought made her sparkle and skip down the hallway at school.

"Guess what?" Marisa asked Rene after she gave him a hug, planning to tell him about her unfounded cancer scare.

"Not now." Rene shushed her by pressing a finger across her mouth and tugged her away from streams of students kicking down the hallway. They fled to the empty baseball diamond, where he unzipped his backpack and pulled out a tabby kitten whose eyes were half shut. The cat yawned and its tiny legs pedaled in the air.

"Qué linda," Marisa cooed.

Rene had to agree. He told her that he had found the kitten on the way to school.

"What are you going to do with her?"

"Keep her."

"But, I mean, we're in school."

Rene pulled back the sleeve of his shirt and checked the time. It was 8:12 and first period didn't start until 8:35.

"I'll keep her in my backpack," Rene said, but then decided that was probably an unwise move. Not all the teachers were old and deaf, so surely one of them would pick up the sound of meowing. They opted to hide the kitten on campus. "But we're going to need some food. She's, like, starving."

Marisa suggested the 7-Eleven on Fruit Avenue, and they were off, the cat meowing and Marisa meowing back. She had had a cat when she was very young, but the cat, a homebody who slept on an army blanket on the back porch, disappeared one day. She had made her dad drive around the block, her head hanging out the car window and crying, "Princess, Princess, where are you?" She remembered the rain and the reflection of her teary face, distorted in the wet car window. It didn't help that her father had quipped, "It's going to rain cats and dogs, and you'll get another cat—you'll see."

"Don't worry, baby kitty-kitty," Marisa sang as she let go of that sorrowful memory. "We're going to save you, kitty-witty." Then, patting her hip, she said, "Feel this."

Rene touched her hip—politely, as if he were a doctor.

"What do you feel?"

"It's your hip bone," he said, unmoved. "What about it?"

"When I got out of the shower this morning, I thought this bumpy bone was cancer. I'd never noticed it before. But I'm okay!" She hugged Rene and petted his backpack. "We're going to save you, kitty-witty."

They bought a can of cat food. Outside the store Marisa pulled back the tab, and the can opened with a sigh. She stuck her finger into the food and forked out a glob.

"Here's some grub." Marisa beckoned. She wiggled her finger at the kitten, which Rene had set on the curb. The cat, dazed by sunlight and freedom, staggered, stumbled, and rose to sniff a dandelion.

"It's *comida* time," Marisa crowed as she set the kitten on her lap.

The kitten poked at her finger and licked it, then began to suckle it.

"It's so hungry," Marisa whined pitifully. She dipped her finger into the cat food for a second helping.

They fed the kitten, returned it to the backpack, and started back to school in a hurry—they were late. On the way they faced a problem larger than if the vice principal had called them into the office.

"It's my mom!" Rene cried, and stepped away from Marisa.

His mother's car had just turned a corner, slowed, and braked in the middle of the road, its taillights red as sin. She whipped her head around, and her eyes locked on them. The car window rolled down.

"What are you two up to?" she yelled.

They turned and hurried through the broken fence at the corner of the campus. Marisa was miffed at Rene for having stepped away from her. She was aware that he wasn't brave, but wasn't she his girlfriend? Was he *that* scared of his mother?

"I'm sorry I did that," Rene apologized. He had picked up on her disappointment. He tried to put his hand around her waist, but she shrugged him off.

They walked in silence, ignoring the cat's meowing. When they began to cross the baseball field, Marisa asked, "What are we going to do with the cat?"

Rene suggested the dugout by the baseball diamond. "She won't go anywhere," he said. He set the can of cat food on the floor of the dugout, and the kitten licked it.

"She's so cute," Marisa said in a brighter mood as she took Rene's hand in hers. She didn't want to stay grumpy. It wasn't his fault his mother's second vehicle was a broom. She rested her head against his shoulder and scanned the school grounds—a landlocked seagull, wing raised, was pecking at its feathers. "I wish we could go far away."

"Like where?" Rene asked.

"To the ocean. Or maybe to somewhere it snows."

Rene embraced and kissed Marisa. "That would be okay with me."

"Wouldn't it be cool if that seagull got really, really big so that we could sit on it and fly away?" Marisa became dreamy as she envisioned both of them clinging to the neck of the seagull and flapping along at cloud level.

"It's possible," Rene said. "One day it's going to happen."

"What do you mean?"

"Gene research. In a decade scientists are going to be able to increase the size of animals. You just watch."

"Maybe you'll be one of the scientists."

Marisa expanded on the dream of flying away on the back of a seagull. They would live on an island, drink coconut milk, and skewer fish on sticks and roast them over an open fire. She told Rene that when their clothes shredded to nothing, they could weave themselves hula skirts and make sandals out of tree bark. And if they got sick, they could lie on the beach and let the sun heal them.

"What about the kitten?" Rene asked.

"We'll take her with us." Marisa tickled the kitten's chin. "Huh, silly? You'll go with us to a faraway island. There will be a boy kitty waiting for you."

"What should we name her?" Rene asked.

Marisa was quick with an answer. She liked the name Sammy, short for Samantha, but didn't explain that she had seen the name with a heart drawn on the chalkboard in the storage room. She didn't divulge the story about the girl who had died and was forgotten.

They were late for their first classes and walked hand in hand, as if they were handcuffed, into the principal's office.

But the principal had no time for them. The secretary presented them with tardy slips and shooed them out the door. There was an emergency. One of the students in art class had sliced his wrist and showered blood all over the classroom. By first break everyone was talking about Cody, the boy who had taken a shard of glass and raked it over his wrist.

"Do you know him?" Marisa asked as they hurried across the field toward the baseball diamond.

"Not really," Rene answered. "I just remember

him from fourth grade. He put a crayon up his nose, and they had to call the fire department to get it out."

"Nah!"

"I'm serious. They had to call the fire department."

Marisa pictured a red crayon sticking out of the kid's nose. She couldn't help but think that had been a sign of worse things yet to come—red nose, red wrist.

They found the kitten asleep on the bench in the dugout.

"Sammy!" Marisa called. She bent down and picked up the cross-eyed cat—it had been sleeping and was still groggy. She cradled the kitten in her arms but handed it to Rene when her cell phone rang.

"Yeah," Marisa said. It was Priscilla calling from somewhere on campus.

Marisa was excited to share the secret about the kitten. But Priscilla had a secret of her own. She said that a boy—a good-looking one, too—was shadowing her. Their faces had almost touched when they bent down at the water fountain at the same time. And he had been two places behind her when she was in line to get a *churro*. Didn't that mean something?

"You go, girl!" Marisa exclaimed. "The stars are

aligned and coming together. You were meant to be a couple!" When Marisa was younger, she had followed her horoscope closely and believed that the moon and the stars had an effect on mankind. (She was a whimsical Sagittarius, given to flights of fancy and temper tantrums.) She had never, however, read, "A nerd will come into your life." Some events were inexplicable, like the discovery of the kitten, which was now on top of Rene's shoes throwing jabs at the laces. Neither could Marisa explain why Priscilla had already forgotten Aaron, but she was glad about it.

"Even the cat doesn't like my shoes," Rene joked.

"They are ugly, *muy feos,*" Marisa agreed. "It would be better if you went barefoot."

"I almost am." He stood storklike and lifted one leg to present with pride the bottom of one of his shoes—there was a small worn hole in the sole.

When the bell rang, Marisa stroked the kitten good-bye and promised to return. She and Rene hurried across the baseball field but slowed to a stop when they heard Adam and Brittany, Romeo and Juliet in the play, arguing viciously. Adam was calling Brittany self-centered and Brittany, her face just inches from his, was calling Adam a thoughtless brat for not remembering her birthday.

Marisa had not known that they were a couple.

It was one more surprise for the day—a kitten that belonged to them and then a spat between boyfriend and girlfriend. She could tell right there, in center field where many a baseball had been caught and dropped, that this Romeo wouldn't die for his Juliet—not a chance. As for Juliet, she wouldn't chug down any poison for this lover boy. Life was too precious.

They sped off when Juliet started to jab a fingernail into Romeo's shoulder. She was making a point that Marisa didn't care to know.

It was enchilada night at home, and after dinner it was Marisa's duty to bust the suds on the pile of greasy plates and pans. She loved her enchiladas, especially red cheesy ones, but also hated those evenings. She often changed the water twice to get the plates to come clean.

It had been a heartbreaking day, too. When she and Rene returned after school to claim the kitten, it was gone. Marisa's eyes had become moist, and her lower lip trembled for Sammy. The seagull was gone as well. For a moment as they walked across the baseball field, hand in hand with their heads bowed from their loss, Marisa had imagined that the kitten was on the back of the seagull and headed somewhere nice.

"Mom," Marisa called softly.

Her mother was searching the pantry for a can of tuna for the next day's lunch. She came out with a can of SPAM. "What?" she asked.

"Are you going to come to see *Romeo and Juliet*?"

"*Claro.* I'll be seated right up front." She nudged her daughter away from the sink to rinse the top of the can. She dried the can on her apron and asked, "Who's this boy you like? He comes over here to play chess, but you never talk about him."

Marisa's face reddened, not from the steamy dishwater but from her mother's direct question. Had she dropped clues about having a boyfriend? Maybe her mom had guessed from Marisa's sudden weight loss. With nowhere to turn in their small kitchen, Marisa had provided her mother with the truth: Yes, she had a boyfriend and, yes, it was that boy who had come over—Rene, the certified nerd.

Her mother gazed at her daughter, measuring the truth.

"You're not going to do anything serious with him, right?" she finally asked.

The directness of the question shamed Marisa. "No!" She liked holding hands and hugging and taking his breath away with kisses. But she was not ready for anything riskier.

Marisa's mother studied her for a minute, then turned away without offering a lecture about boys and girls. She mumbled something about misplaced black olives as she began to look in the refrigerator.

"Is Dad coming, too?" Marisa was eager to change the subject.

"¿Cómo?" her father called from the living room. He was seated in his recliner for the evening, a hand on the remote in order to mute the volume when a commercial began to blabber.

"Dad!" she screamed. "Do you want to see me in *Romeo and Juliet*?" She had set the last pan on the dish rack.

"¿Cómo?" he brayed.

Marisa finished by wiping the counter, and she and her mother joined her father in the living room. *Monday Night Football* was on, and her father was resting his bones while the players on the screen were throwing themselves at each other viciously.

"The play's this week. I don't have a speaking part, but I'm in the chorus."

"You're in a play?" her father asked in disbelief.

Marisa remained patient. "In *Romeo and Juliet*. Remember? I told you over dinner, and you said you had a girlfriend, before Mom, named Julieta?"

Her father turned in confusion to Marisa's

mother, who said, "*Viejo,* you're going to a play. And you never had a *novia* except me."

Her father smiled and said, "Oh, that's right." He had the recliner leaned back like a dentist chair but worked a lever on the side that brought him sitting straight up.

"You gonna be in a play?" he repeated after a while. "I can't believe it—an actress." He drummed his fingers on the arm of the recliner.

By the goofy smile on his face, Marisa could see that he was proud of her. She had sat down with her mother on the couch but suddenly stood and announced, "I'm going to sing my part for you." She positioned herself in front of the television, muted for her performance, and began to sing as her father once again reclined, eyes shut, feet moving left and right to the rhythm of the song. There was a smile on his weary face, and every now and then he would open his eyes—she realized that he couldn't help it—to take a peek at the game. "He's a good father," she told herself. She sang the chorus part and then moved aside a few inches. One of her daughterly duties was to not get in the way of a father and his football game.

Chapter

"My mom pinched me right here." Rene stopped their hand-in-hand trek across the baseball field to unbutton his long-sleeved shirt so Marisa could see the bruise. Eventually it would fade, but then it stood out dark and sore. It was early morning before first period. They were on their way to do one more search for Sammy.

"Mom said again that she doesn't want me to see you." Rene confirmed her suspicions—his mother feared that she would drag her son down. Marisa presumed that in Rene's mother's eyes she was nothing but a low-class *chola*.

"I'm not a bad person," Marisa insisted. As she began to fill with meanness, she checked herself and defused her anger against Rene's mother. Yes, she thought it was unfair. Rene's mother didn't know anything about her. How did she know Marisa would get in the way of her son's progress? He might go to Harvard or Stanford, but she might tag along with her own stupendous grades and test scores.

"Do you want to break up with me?" Marisa asked. Her eyes flooded. She had to wonder if they would remain flooded through first period and beyond. The night before, in bed, she had cried about the loss of Sammy and, for comfort, had brought out from her bottom drawer her old stuffed unicorn with the bent horn.

"No," he answered. "If I did, who would tell me what kind of pants to wear?"

She latched her arms around his waist and kissed him, her very own personal nerd. For her he was superior to a *cholo* boy any day. Before she had come to Hamilton Magnet, her anger would have flashed like a struck match and she would have closed her hands into fists. Now she felt not anger but a sadness that was deep as a river. She couldn't explain why Rene was the way he was, including that honking laugh of his. She would take him with his awful-looking clothes, his nerdy friends, his schemes of tutoring others in search of money. But she had to wonder if maybe he would be bolder if his father had been a part of his life. She conjured up the *vatos* at her old school parading their badness. Rene, she concluded, needed a little of their juice, a little of their bravado.

They didn't find the cat or the seagull.

"She's gone," Marisa cried.

"I'll find another kitten," Rene promised. "A really pretty one. Just you watch."

All morning Marisa couldn't concentrate on her classes—she worked a pen quietly across her binder, her mind drifting. Then, during first break, Priscilla introduced the boy who had been following her—it was the skateboarder who had taunted Rene.

"Hi," said the skateboarder, whose name was Erik. Marisa could tell that he remembered her. He might even have remembered Marisa's outburst when he had called Rene a doofus. Erik was wearing fingerless black gloves, and his skateboard, pasted with stickers, was under his arm. His hair was still dyed green.

"We gotta go," Priscilla said. She looked up at Erik, blushing, and all indications were that she liked him a lot.

"She's picked a grungy dude," Marisa told herself. They disappeared among the crowd, and from that same crowd appeared Rene.

"I just saw Priscilla," Marisa said. "Remember that guy who called you doofus?"

"No, I don't remember." They were heading toward the secret room in the abandoned part of the gym.

"What do you mean? He was riding his skateboard and we were sitting over there." She pointed to a bench, where three girls in long leather coats and net stockings sat polishing their fingernails black.

"People call me names all the time," Rene explained. "Or they used to. I can't remember them all." He changed the subject and took her hands in his. He began talking rapidly about the debate team that was forming, but Marisa was not listening. She loved Rene more than ever, all because he appeared helpless. She knew that usually the guy protected the girl—or at least that was what she had salvaged from the story lines of teenage romances. But their roles were reversed. It was she who opened the door to the gym, she who held his feet when he did sit-ups, she who spotted him when he lay grunting on the bench press—he could now lift sixty pounds

He did three chin-ups, legs bicycling as he struggled to get his chin up to the bar, and followed that with a set of bench presses and a single set of curls for his biceps. For Marisa, her exercise was to lift him into her arms and carry him out the door. She let him slip from her arms when they got outside.

"I think—really!—that I've gotten stronger," Rene remarked.

"I noticed some little hills in your arms." She asked him to show her his biceps, and she squeezed his small, round muscle. It wasn't rock hard, but neither did it feel like a water balloon. There was some muscle beneath the skin.

After school Rene, giddy with excitement, coaxed Marisa aside and said, "Look at this. I did this in calculus."

When he started to roll up his sleeve, she thought that he was going to show her another bruise. She was ready to chant a litany of bad words and sting that mean mother for hurting her boy. Instead, Marisa saw her name inked on his slender forearm. Her name was in a heart, and her mind leaped back to the chalkboard with the heart around the name *Samantha.*

"I'm going to get a tattoo here when I turn seventeen," he announced proudly. "In four years. I'll be old enough then."

In four years? she wondered, and began to do the math in her head.

"How old are you?" she asked. She was fourteen and would be fifteen in January.

"I'm thirteen. I skipped a grade because, you know—"

"Thirteen!" she screamed, her chewing gum nearly shooting out of her mouth.

"But I'm mature for my age," he claimed.

"Nah, you're not. You're my beautiful egghead. My little *huevito* head." She touched the ink tattoo on his arm.

He wagged his head and honked his funny laugh. He agreed that he was an egghead with plenty of smarts upstairs.

They walked toward the auditorium for drama rehearsal, Marisa secretly dazed by the fact that her boyfriend was younger than she. Oh, now he would really have her protection. She would scratch, kick, spit, and pull hair for her dude. No bully was going to push him around anymore. If by some unlucky chance a car should fall on him, she would beat her chest like King Kong and lift it off him. There was nothing that she would not do. She would even catch up to him in math and, in the evenings, while sipping a shared soda, they would explore complicated equations. In her veins swam a large dose of love.

Marisa instructed Rene to stand on the other side of the chorus of sixteen students during rehearsal. When he asked why, she told him she wanted to view him from a different angle. She longed to cast smiles and kisses and see him from the distance of a few feet. And he had better not flirt with the girl next to him—she raised a claw and hissed.

"You like me, huh?" he asked.

"Mucho," she confessed.

They entered the auditorium to find Romeo and Juliet fighting onstage.

"My mom took my cell phone away," Rene moaned into the telephone that evening.

"Where are you?" Marisa had fallen asleep on the couch with a math book on her lap. Her father was also asleep in his recliner, the remote control in his hand and the television muted. Her mother was nowhere about. She said to Rene, "Wait a minute."

Marisa got up and took the call on the front porch after slipping into flip-flops. She shivered in the cool autumn air.

"Where are you?" she repeated.

"I'm calling from home. Mom's in the shower." He told her that he had never been so down. "I don't think she likes me. She says she wants me to succeed, but she's mean about it."

"Why don't you tell your father?" Marisa suggested.

There was silence. Finally, he answered, "I don't know."

They talked for a while and Marisa let Rene repeat himself, how he wished he could be old enough to go away to college. In college he would have new friends and a place of his own, even if it were only a shared bedroom in a noisy dorm.

"I'll go with you," Marisa said. She pictured herself and Rene driving a car to college. "We can be with each other."

"You can help me pick my clothes," he said, trying to lighten the moment.

But the mood was dark as the sky. They talked for a few minutes, and then he said he had to go—the shower had stopped.

"I know she's trying to break us up, but she's not going to do it." Rene hung up without a good-bye.

Marisa remained on the porch, leaning against the rail. She couldn't register the emotion inside her. It was close to loneliness, yet not loneliness. It was sadness, yet not sadness. She pocketed her cell phone and walked down the porch steps to retrieve the free weekly newspaper no one ever read.

She gazed up at the night sky, rubbing her arms and shivering. The stars appeared to be pulsating a silvery light, and the moon was nowhere in sight. She had read her horoscope that morning while eating a bowl of Cheerios with thin slices of banana. The horoscope predicted travel and changes in friendships. She remembered laughing and thinking, *Yeah, right,* and rattling the box of Cheerios as she debated if she should have a second bowl. She had decided against it, though she devoured a second banana.

"Poor Rene." She caught herself crying under the night sky. "Poor baby." She chanted Rene's name, retrieved the newspaper, and returned inside, where she stirred the shoulder of her sleeping father and whispered into his ear, "It's time for bed, *Papi.*"

The horoscope was true in its prediction. Marisa would travel, but not too far. There would be new friends—sort of. The next day at school, Mr. Laird, the counselor, called her into his office and informed her that she had to return to her old school because she didn't live in the Hamilton district. His large hands were like gavels on his desk, and after a moment of staring he offered a light reprimand for using her aunt's address on her registration.

"But you wouldn't like the school I had to go to! They slash teachers' cars at that stupid school!"

Mr. Laird ignored Marisa's outburst.

"How did you find out?" she asked.

"We just found out."

Maybe Rene's mother told him, she thought. Was it possible? Was his mom that desperate?

Marisa was escorted from Mr. Laird's office by the secretary. She waited in a room where copy machines hummed and the janitor came in periodically to search through the cabinets.

Her mother arrived an hour later, sparks nearly chipping off her high heels when she was led into the room where her daughter sat, legs splayed and arms crossed over her chest. Marisa's posture said everything—she was mad! In turn, her mother was even madder. She scolded the counselor, then spent some of her wrath on the vice principal. Right then Marisa could see that she was like her mother. Her mother let words fire and hit the school staff where they stood.

While Marisa had sat in the room waiting, she'd mused on what she could only call her misfortune. When she risked a cell phone call to Rene's house, his mother picked up and told her that he was ill in bed. She was hostile and warned her to leave her son alone.

Now this showdown at school.

"There are policies!" the vice principal claimed sternly. He was a man who dealt daily with students and parents, and knew when to raise and lower his voice. The moment called upon him to hitch up his pants and defend his school.

Marisa's mother waved him off and led her daughter outside to the parking lot. They got into the car and drove away.

"That stupid school," her mother barked, knuckles white from her hard grip on the steering wheel.

"But Mom, we don't live in the school district. Mr. Laird is right." All the anger had left Marisa; she just felt defeated. She sat with her hands laced on her lap and didn't give any credence to her mother's illogical tirade: This was America and her daughter could go to any school she pleased.

Marisa let her mother speak her mind because her own mind was on Rene. Sure, they would see each other on the sly, but she would miss seeing him daily. She started weeping and turned away when her mother offered her a Kleenex. She stared out the car window until the nice neighborhood around Hamilton slowly gave way to homes that were not so nice.

By third period Marisa was at her old school, sitting in an English class where the students were asleep, talking, or looking out a window scarred with names scrawled on it. The teacher, Mrs. Pacheco, was discussing *another* Robert Frost poem set in snow, although no one among them had ever seen snow. Ice, yes, ice in Big Gulps and sodas of various flavors. But snow falling from the sky and whitening the world with a fresh look? An absolute no.

There, in a wobbly chair in the third row, Marisa could see that she wasn't going to go far. She might never see snow. She might never know another kind of life. In a way the horoscope of the previous day was a lie.

Chapter

So it was back to Washington, back to the crowds kicking down the narrow throat of poorly lit hallways, back to girls dipping their fingers into potato chip bags and throwing their heads back as if everything was funny. Back to the earsplitting laughter, the shouts of, "Girl, what you mean!" and the roll of Spanish from Mexicano boys who, three months before, had been country boys but were now suddenly urban *vatos.* The Vietnamese boys with spiky hair threw sideways glances like darts. *It's noisy here,* Marisa thought at lunchtime. When she found one of her feet in a puddle of spilled soda, she grimaced and stepped out of the syrupy glaze and advanced a few steps in the cafeteria line. She paid for a bag of potato chips (she couldn't help breaking her vow to stay away from junk food), left the commotion of the lunchroom, and headed out toward the front of the school, a quiet sanctuary. Security guards paced in front.

Marisa had to wonder how this move had happened. Only a few hours before she'd been at Hamilton Magnet, and then there she was at Washington, ripping open a bag of barbecue-flavored potato chips. She had attracted a single pigeon, but that pigeon beat its crooked wings and flew to a group of students having lunch at a far bench.

"I don't care," she remarked wistfully as she raised a chip to her mouth and began to chew without tasting the barbecue flavor. She watched the cars pass beyond the fence and pedestrians stroll, hurry, gallop, and run down the sidewalk. *La chota* cruised past like a shark waiting to bite, and a UPS truck pulled up, braked, and turned on its hazard lights. For a moment she imagined that the muscled UPS driver was delivering more potato chips, the preferred food group of this school. But he was pushing a dolly loaded with boxes of textbooks.

It was a busy world beyond the fence and a lonely place where she sat. She wished she could write a song and sing it. She had discovered at Hamilton Magnet that she possessed a good singing voice. The choir director had smiled at her when her voice stretched, and wasn't that a sign that the voice inside was pretty? "I'm in a place," she sang, "in a place..." But that's as far as she got before her made-up song faltered.

Across the lawn she spied Alicia and Roberto sitting on the edge of the school fountain, a gift from one of the classes long ago when the school had been white and money had appeared like leaves on a tree. Now the fountain was turned off and was used mostly as a garbage can—cups and wrappers, bottles, old gym socks, Popsicle sticks, splintered Bic pens, poorly spelled notes, a binder, Valentine cards from the year before, and other debris lay in a moat of rust-colored water.

Marisa buried her face in her hands. She couldn't bring herself to talk to Alicia yet. Maybe it wasn't true about her and Roberto. Maybe they were just talking one last time, but when she peeked through her fingers she could see they were holding hands. And was that the sparkle of a ring on Alicia's finger? Had she forgiven that rat? How could she?

"I'm not going to be like them," she muttered. It was a vague promise, one that she knew she couldn't explain even to herself. She poured her potato chips onto the ground, and the pigeon that had been working the group of other students returned to feed on the spicy calories that would keep it warm under its bent feathers.

Barrio bird, she thought. *Poor barrio bird. Poor all of us.*

Marisa knew she would still remain friends with Alicia. They had known each other for years. What harm had Alicia done to her? That she had picked a sorry-ass boyfriend wasn't her fault. But maybe they just wouldn't be *best* friends anymore.

Marisa got up and returned to the main quad, where she encountered Latisha, who screamed, "What you doin' here? You spyin', huh?"

Marisa gave Latisha a light hug. "They caught me and sent me back across the border."

"And look at you!" Latisha had stepped back. "You, like, lost weight. You sick o' something?"

"No, just trying to get one of them." Marisa threw a hitchhiker's thumb at three guys headed toward the gym.

Latisha and Latisha's friends sang like a chorus: "We hear ya."

Marisa didn't take more than three steps before she dismissed her proclamation as an utter lie. She had lost weight for herself, not for some boy on his way to shoot baskets. She didn't care what those stupid boys thought. Why did they play during lunch and then bounce to class when lunchtime was over? Didn't they know they smelled funky after ten minutes? No, she had lost weight for herself and, yes, for Rene.

The day was a bumpy ride from class to class, and that afternoon she was glad to get home. She went to her bedroom and cried onto the tiny shoulder of her stuffed animal. She slipped into her pajamas, finished with the day. She was tired and hungry. Tears would roll again later when she lay in bed recounting the vice principal's scolding accusations hurled at her mother.

Marisa scrutinized the clock—4:15. Rene would be at rehearsal and singing like a bird. She was waiting for him to return home. Rene's mother would have sent him back to school after she figured out that Marisa, the *chola,* had gone away.

She heard her cell phone ring.

"Rene?" she asked, heart thumping.

"Yeah, it's me."

"Where are you? I thought your mom took your cell away."

Rene told her that he was using Trung's cell phone, that he was in the parking lot at school, and that he had only a few minutes before his mother picked him up.

"They sent me away," Marisa blubbered. She almost added that she thought that it was his mother who had called the school and ratted on her.

"My mom was really mad."

Marisa could hear him start crying. His crying sounded like his honking laughter.

"Rene, stop that!" Marisa scolded.

"I can't help it. Wait a minute."

Marisa could hear him honking into his handkerchief. She had to smile. He was the only boy she knew who pocketed a clean handkerchief at the start of the day.

"I think my mom is the one who turned you in. She asked me a lot about you, and I ended up telling her where you live. I'll call you whenever I can." He blew kisses into the cell phone and then hung up.

Marisa was touched. His friend and main opponent in chess had been standing at his side and had witnessed Rene's words of love.

That night after dinner Marisa's father kept the television off in protest of his daughter's being expelled from Hamilton Magnet. He looked so much like a sad mule that Marisa considered patting his tanned forearm to say, "It's okay, *Papi.* I'm gonna live."

He sipped his coffee and finally spoke up. "It's better this way. You'll do good, *mi'ja.*" He began his story about the treks from school to school when he was young. His parents were migrant farmworkers who worked crops in Oregon and Washington, and in California's Central Valley. Using his thick fingers, he counted sixteen schools, including one called Washington and another called Hamilton. He sighed as he finished his coffee.

But her mother was still fuming. She sat on the couch and, by the light of a dim lamp, worked furiously as she knitted what looked like a hangman's noose. Marisa swallowed. Was she really making a noose? If so, the vice principal—what was his name?—would at least hang in a noose made of soft wool.

"How dare they!" her mother snarled at her father.

"Why scold me? I agree with you." He rolled his fingers on the arm of the recliner and reached for the remote control but put it back down. This was going to be an evening of silence. The only noise came from the rapid clicking sounds of the knitting needles.

But Marisa made noise, too. Her noise came from turning the pages of her biology book. For her it was a time to learn.

The next week brought showers that stripped trees

of leaves and weaker branches and had her father climbing the neighbor's roof to patch a leak. Autumn was giving way to winter in their valley town.

Mornings, Marisa found herself shivering over the heater vent in the floor, her pajama bottoms billowing about her. She was worried about how upset Rene was, and was relieved when he called on Trung's cell phone to say—Marisa grimaced at the old-fashioned phrase—everything was hunky-dory.

"Are you sure?" she asked. She was convinced that he was okay when he started his honking laughter as he described an unplanned scene in *Romeo and Juliet* at the premiere—Juliet had pushed and slapped Romeo onstage. Juliet's jealous rage had erupted when Romeo lovingly stroked the cheek of Lady Capulet, Juliet's mother.

Then silence over the weekend. Another storm rolled in and brought down a power line that made them sit in the dark of their living room. Her father sat sleeping in his recliner, a hibernating bear. Her mother continued knitting not a noose, as Marisa had imagined, but a sweater for her niece's forthcoming baby. The niece was sixteen, only a year and some months older than Marisa.

On Monday, Marisa woke up with a sore throat and considered asking her mother if she could stay home. But she got dressed, shimmying into a dress she hadn't worn in months, ate her breakfast, and instead of walking the six blocks to school, accepted a ride from her mother because it had started to rain hard. She angled a beret on her head and reddened her lips with lipstick.

"You look so cute in that hat," her mother said brightly as she wiped the inside of the fogged windshield with an old T-shirt she kept under the seat for such use.

"Thanks, Mom."

But she didn't feel cute as her mind dwelled on school. She had encountered Alicia with and without an unrepentant Roberto. The two girls were friendly but not close. Mostly, Marisa kept to herself. What friends she had had before avoided her now—the rumor was that she transferred to Hamilton Magnet because she was stuck-up but couldn't hang there because the classes were too hard.

Before driving to school, her mother swung by her niece's house. Marisa hardly saw her cousin except at Christmas. They dropped off the sweater, and the cousin, barefoot on the porch, waved goodbye. A child bride, she was wearing pajamas printed with Disney characters.

Marisa was surprised her mother hadn't made a remark such as, "I hope that doesn't happen to you." No, her mother drove with both hands on the steering wheel, her face pushed forward as she peered through the windshield, which kept fogging up no matter how hard the defroster blew. The rain came down harder.

At school her mother leaned over and gave Marisa a kiss. "You have a good day. *Qué linda, mi'ja.* You look so cute."

Marisa got out of the car, waved, and touched the place where her mother had placed the kiss. Her mother hadn't kissed her like that in years.

Because she was early, Marisa ventured into the library, where she noticed a boy with crooked glasses. For a heartbeat she thought it was Rene. But the boy was too short, and the boy next to him even shorter. They were playing chess on a magnetic board. Both, she noticed, had high-water pants and white socks.

Nerds, she thought. *Eggheads.*

Marisa sat down and opened her English text-book. The book was the same one she'd used at Hamilton Magnet. She turned to read the Robert Frost poem about snow, her lips moving over every third word. It was the quietness of the snow that at-tracted her. As she gazed up at the high windows of the library, she wished that the rain would flatten into snowflakes. She was reading the poem again when a voice called, "A penny for your thoughts."

She turned. Rene stood there in a long black coat.

"Rene?"

He shrugged. "I guess."

"What are you doing here?" She rose from her chair and walked into his coat, which had opened like bat wings. They hugged and kissed, and she remarked that he smelled like coffee.

"I drank a cup at breakfast. I'm living with my dad now."

"You are?" Marisa was delirious with excitement. She would have burst into a snowflake if it were possible. "But how? Why didn't you tell me?"

"I wanted to surprise you. Are you surprised?"

"Yeah, I am," she cooed. "I missed you so much."

They sat down at the table, aware that the librarian had cast an eye at them, and spoke in whispers. Rene began by saying that his father took him in—he shared a large home with his girlfriend, which was in the Washington High School district.

"You got a transfer!"

Rene nodded. He described the last argument with his mother and how she had hit him. He had run out of the house and walked six miles to his father's home.

"I don't blame Dad for leaving us anymore." He described the showdown between his mother and father later that evening at his dad's house. His father's defense tactic was to keep the screen door locked and let his ex-wife scream and claw the screen like a wild cat. She threatened to take him to court, and he threatened her by saying that he was going to take photographs of Rene's bruises and scratches—he had new ones on his arms and face. The police, he said, would love such fine examples of motherly love.

Marisa squeezed his hand and then released it to search for a Kleenex in her backpack. But Rene was quick to pick up his cue, snapping his handkerchief from his back pocket.

They stared at each other, Marisa glancing every few seconds at the clock on the wall. They had six minutes before first period.

"Rene," she meowed. "Rene, you look so different."

"Dad bought me new clothes." He clicked his boots together. "What do you think? You look marvelous in your beret."

"Thank you." She spied his boots from under the table. "They're nice." She wiped her eyes again with the handkerchief. "But I think you're going to have to do something with your glasses." They were fogged up from the heat of the library and—she knew this was also true—the heat that could only be love.

"I'm going to like it here," he said, lifting his eyebrows and jerking his head toward the boys playing chess.

Marisa turned and was moved momentarily by a flutter of shame. She had never acknowledged those two boys. She had seen them in the hallways, sometimes bouncing off older and stronger students, but she had never really noticed them. They hadn't been part of her world. She dabbed her eyes again.

"Hey, I have an idea. We'll start our own chess team, our own debate team, whatever kind of club you want," Marisa suggested.

"We can do *Romeo and Juliet.*"

"If you wish."

They got up, Marisa adjusting her beret, and together they strolled over to the two boys. The smaller boy pushed his eyeglasses up on his face. He seemed to already know Rene, and Rene started to suggest a move on the board but remained quiet.

Marisa witnessed the meeting of those minds. *Dang,* she thought. *These nerds recognize each other! They know their own kind!*

When the bell rang for first period, Marisa and Rene gathered their backpacks. They left the library and nearly slipped on the steps. It was snowing, a first for the valley town, and Marisa was crazy with happiness as she turned and turned, arms out and mouth opening to catch flakes.

"I can't believe it," Rene shouted as he, too, twirled and his long coat flared. He slipped, fell, and rose again.

"It's really snowing, Rene!" Marisa was spellbound, her cheeks burning pink in the cold. "It's happening in our lifetime—snow in our little town! Can you believe it!"

They ran out to the football field, where they skidded and fell and brought their faces together for kisses, the taste of snowflakes on their lips.

Selected Spanish Words and Phrases

albóndigas	meatballs in broth
arroz	rice
ay, Chihuahua	oh, my
beso	kiss
cálmate	calm down
chale	no way
chavalos	youngsters
chicharrones	fried pork rinds
cholo/a	gangster
churro	Mexican doughnut
claro	of course
cochino	pig
comida	food
cómo	how/what
el mero mero	the top guy
es muy firme	it's way cool
ese vato	that guy
estúpido	stupid

gabacho	white person
güey	idiot
hermanas	sisters
hombre	man
huevito	small egg
la chota	the police
la crema	the cream
la rata	the rat
los frijoles	the beans
los pantalones	pants
mala	bad
mentiroso/a	liar
mi'ja	my daughter
mi jefita took *mis llaves*	my old lady took my keys
mira	look
mi ranfla	my cool car
mis tías	my aunts
mucho	a lot
muy fea/feos	very ugly
nerdito	little nerd
novia	girlfriend
novio	boyfriend
papi	daddy
pata	leg
pedos	farts
pendejo	dummy
pleitos	fights

pobrecita	poor little girl
qué gacho, carnal	what a drag, buddy
qué linda	how pretty/cute
qué no	isn't that so?
queso de cotija	cotija cheese
recuerdas	do you remember?
refritos	refried
sapo	toad
siempre	always
tonto	fool
tú sabes	you know
una gordita	a fat little girl
ven	come here
verdad	right?
viejo	old man
y qué más	and what else?